EARLY PRAISE FOR MYLO CARBIA

"Sorry, Hollywood. Looks like 'The Queen of Horror' is blowing up the literary world and you won't be able to woo her back."

– Latino LA Hollywood

"A breathtaking story, fast-paced, insanely vivid – just brilliant!"

– Roberts Book Reviews, Australia

"Horror's next *New York Times* bestseller."

– All Indie Magazine

"It's the way Carbia weaves this horror tale that makes this book truly shine."

– Gotham News

"She's the next Stephen King."

ety

THE
RAPING
OF
AVA
DESANTIS

Coming Soon From Mylo Carbia

VIOLETS ARE RED

YORUBA

Z.O.O.

THY BE SHUNNED

DAUGHTERS OF MARIE LAVEAU

TERLINGUA

ROCKEFELLER
PUBLISHING GROUP

45 Rockefeller Plaza, Suite 2000, New York, NY 10111 USA
www.RockefellerPublishing.com

THE
RAPING
OF
AVA
DESANTIS

A Horror Novel

MYLO CARBIA

ABOUT THE AUTHOR

Mylo Carbia is an American screenwriter and author best known for her work in the horror, thriller and science fiction genres.

Born and raised in Jackson, New Jersey, Carbia spent her childhood years writing to escape the horrors of growing up in a haunted house. As the daughter of "The Prince of Mambo" Eddie Carbia and goddaughter of the late actor Raul Julia, Carbia was surrounded by the entertainment industry from an early age.

By the age of 17, she was already well established as a prolific young playwright. At the age of 21, Carbia wrote, produced and directed *The Dolly Parton Conspiracy*, winner of the Troubadour Theatrical Society's Best Play Award in 1992.

At the age of 30, her very first screenplay was optioned only 28 days after completion, earning Carbia a "three picture deal" and the cover of *Hollywood Scriptwriter* in October 2003. After that time, Carbia quietly penned numerous television and film projects under her production company Zohar Films – earning the nickname "The Queen of Horror" and the reputation of being Hollywood's No. 1 horror film ghostwriter.

In 2014, Carbia announced BIG plans to leave ghostwriting and move into the literary world to write a series of bestselling horror, thriller and science fiction novels all featuring strong female protagonists.

The Raping of Ava DeSantis is her debut novel.

ACKNOWLEDGEMENTS

Special Thanks To:

Pete Tapang for your amazing cover artwork. You are a living master.

Robert McKee for being such a wonderful teacher. You are the master of story.

Jim Dempsey for being a brilliant editor and accepting my writing style with open arms.

Anna Kaiser and the entire AKT InMotion crew for getting me out of my chair at least once a day while I wrote this book.

Sheree Bykofsky, J.E. Fishman, Mike Wells, Carla King, Helen Sedwick and Jeanne Veillette Bowerman for your outstanding advice as I transitioned from film into the literary world.

Lilly Ellison, Michelle Seanez, Pauline Cabrera and Taylor Love for all of your hard work and support in making this book a success.

Arthur Massei for all of your love, support and most of all, *your blessing* to leave Hollywood to write novels. You are an amazing talent manager. Thank you for everything.

Gerard Baker, Michael Gabriel and Antonio Piedra for your belief in my abilities early on as a writer.

Rockefeller Publishing for taking a chance on such a powerful story (and a "genius crazy" writer).

Papo, Kuewpit and Gloria – just know that I am forever grateful! :)

Copyright © 2015 by Mylo Carbia

Published in the United States of America by Rockefeller Publishing Group, Inc.
45 Rockefeller Plaza, Suite 2000, New York, NY 10111 USA
www.RockefellerPublishing.com

Library of Congress Cataloging-in-Publication data is available upon request.

ISBN: 0996565205
ISBN: 9780996565202
eBook ISBN: 9780996565219

Edited by Jim Dempsey
Original cover artwork by Pete Tapang
Author photos by Steven Khan

Mylo Carbia "The Queen of Horror"
305 Broadway, 7th Floor
New York, NY 10007
fans@mylocarbia.com

www.MyloCarbia.com

TWITTER @MyloCarbia
FACEBOOK AuthorMyloCarbia
INSTAGRAM @mylocarbia
GOODREADS mylo_carbia
#RapingAva

www.RapingAva.com

10 9 8 7 6 5 4 3 2 1

First Print Edition

For my *Governor* & *Jett*:

Thank you for loving me just the way I am.

"If an injury has to be done to a man it should be so severe that his vengeance need not be feared."

— Niccolò Machiavelli, *The Prince*, 1532

"No amount of therapy can replace the joy of revenge writing."

— Mylo Carbia, *All Indie Magazine*, 2014

PROLOGUE

Atlanta, Georgia. The city that survived General Sherman's torch in 1864, the death of Martin Luther King in 1968 and the Feline Plague of 2025, symbolizes the humble yet impenetrable warrior strength best embodied by *Atlanta from the Ashes*: a bronze statue of an angel raising a phoenix to the sky in Woodruff Park.

The city's oldest and wealthiest families have most impressively adapted to our ever-changing landscape, morphing from close-minded white plantation owners to migrant worker presidential candidate supporters in less than a millisecond by historical time standards.

But Atlanta's success over the past three hundred years required more than a penchant for resiliency, it depended upon a network of powerful, cunning strategists to stay relevant and alive. Some call it *The Good Ole Boy Network* others consider it remnants of *Confederate Pride*. Whatever one may label it, this cadre of powerful men are responsible for both the birth – and rebirth – of America's most elegant and modern city in the South.

But as any notable historian will tell you...

All of these bastards must die.

CHAPTER 1

WELCOME TO THE MASQUERADE

TUESDAY, OCTOBER 3, 2006
9:46 P.M.

Once a gleaming four-story nightclub catering to Atlanta's mosh-pit-addicted youth, *Le Masquerade* had become a seedy members-only fetish club reduced in size to its former bi-level storage basement with a bustling organic foods market standing above as its pretentious keeper.

Inside, the club was dark, run-down and relatively empty for a weeknight (you know, Fridays for wives, Saturdays for sidepieces and Sundays for confession). On the main floor, a heavily-tattooed stripper danced center stage. She was petite and naked except for a pair of six-inch spike heels and a leather executioner mask with a zipper for a mouth. Her bright yellow eyes behind the mask revealed a vacant spirit, one that was completely immune to the pulsating techno music eroding the rotting plaster surrounding her.

In the audience, sitting alone, was Sebastian O'Connor, a pudgy Southern businessman in his mid-thirties. He would have blended in with the pedestrian audience if it weren't for his armpit-stained Gucci dress shirt contrasting with his perfectly coiffed strawberry blonde hair. Couple that with his near-transparent skin (a shade that bragged a bloodline successful in avoiding the human chattel that once graced his family's hundred-acre farm) and one could tell that this clown was a valid member of local royalty.

Sebastian's affinity for the bondage world started at a young age (eight years old to be exact) when his Jamaican nanny caught him stealing gum from her purse and beat his ass so badly that it stung for hours. It was at this exact time that Sebastian experienced his first erection. Perhaps nothing more than a coincidence but more likely he's been unable to separate the two events ever since.

Add this early experience to the gnawing silence of a drone-at-home wife managing the deafening chaos of three offspring under the age of five, and one can see what drove Sebastian to seek escapism here at least once a week. Fortunately, his role as a hedge fund manager gave him good reason to stay out late entertaining imaginary clients, particularly foreign ones unable to speak English well enough to tour the city on their own.

———⊗∞⊗———

Utterly transfixed by the erotic executioner dance before him, Sebastian felt brazen enough to start touching himself under the table. This was the kind of place where anything goes, except the use of cell phones and cameras, which always had to be surrendered to the green-haired goddess at the front door.

Just as Sebastian began moving clandestinely to unzip his fly, a young, blonde, multi-body-part-pierced waitress interrupted him to serve another shot.

"Need something else?" she slurred. Moving slower than usual, the waitress struggled to add a fresh drink to the shot-glass-graveyard on his table.

Sebastian's attention immediately shifted toward her flawless yet filthy body wrapped tightly in an oxblood leather mini-dress.

"What's your name again, sweetness? My memory's shit."

Lost in her own smack-induced world, the waitress failed to respond. Sebastian suddenly grabbed her pot-holed arm, pulling her body close to his.

"What's your name again?"

"—Jah, Julie."

She stood motionless until Sebastian released his grip, graciously allowing her to continue clearing asshole shot glasses from the table.

"I'm finally ready for some champagne, Jewel-yah."

The waitress mustered all her strength to speak at a normal pace. "Sure...okay...*who* do you want?"

Sebastian looked around the room, carefully considering his options. In one corner, he watched a dark Latino man in pristine white underwear dance for a gay couple...In another, he witnessed an eighty-year old redhead licking the shoes of a young black businessman...And in the roped off VIP section, he noticed a barely legal Japanese schoolgirl performing a lap dance for a local sports anchor slash twice-convicted pedophile.

"Just bring me one of your new girls."

The waitress acknowledged his order, piled the last two empty shot glasses on her overcrowded tray and left as fast as, uh, slow as she could.

At least ten minutes had passed when a tall, thin, elegant woman dressed in full leather gear appeared at Sebastian's table.

"You or-der champagne?" Her deep, velvety voice was contaminated by a thick Russian accent.

"Yes, ma'am. I did."

"Good. I'm Vendela. Follow me."

Sweet Jesus. Sebastian was thrilled to get new blood that's usually sourced from local runaway shelters. But this time, the dominatrix gave the impression that she was an old pro. *Perhaps a visiting artist from another country?* Definitely in her early-thirties, but still in her prime in every way.

Sebastian followed the dominatrix through the main nightclub and into the stairwell. From the back, she strutted an incredible young, tight body. Her thigh-high boots, matching thong and leather suspenders made her the prized snatch of the club. Her long-legged gait was rhythmic and reminiscent of a Clydesdale horse (you know, just like the coke-snorting, seven-figure superstars that glide across the runways of Paris each fall). Naturally, her ass was also perfect. Not too small, not too large but shapely in all of the right places. But what was most intriguing about this woman was the tattoo peeking from underneath her suspenders. It was some sort of large, black tribal symbol that spanned blade to blade across her back. Sebastian could not see the tattoo in detail, nor could he see her face from his vantage point, but he could acutely smell the brand new synthetic, black, bobbed wig and old leather biker cap she was wearing.

The dominatrix led Sebastian down a flight of stairs into *The Dungeon*, which also had the distinct honor of being the most subterranean basement in all of downtown Atlanta. At the bottom, they entered a long dark corridor lined with red curtained stalls. Flickers of candlelight bounced off the ceiling while the faint sound of music from the club upstairs and the new sounds of whips and moaning mixed together in an eerie way.

Sebastian cautiously followed the dominatrix through the corridor to the very last stall, far away from the other patrons. Calm as any other seasoned sex worker, she casually drew back the curtain to reveal a small candlelit room rigged with medieval restraining devices.

For the first time, he was able to see her face. It was long, classically beautiful and ethereal, almost as if she had escaped from an eighteenth century painting. Her high cheekbones and narrow nose were dominated by a set of large, woodsy-green eyes that appeared miles deep with wisdom.

"After you," she said.

Sebastian walked to the middle of the cell, smiling like a spoiled child on Christmas morning.

"Take off your clothes."

Sebastian slowly removed his dress shirt and carefully placed it on the hook located ten steps away.

"Faster, you piece of shit!"

Sebastian's smile quickly faded. He removed his undershirt, belt and pants, throwing each item carelessly off to the side. He stood mildly fearful in the middle of the cell, wearing nothing but his monogramed blue boxer shorts.

"Good. Now turn around. Put your face against wall."

Sebastian complied. The dominatrix slowly shifted behind him, placing his ankles in floor-mounted shackles, then his wrists in wall-mounted handcuffs.

He bent slightly backward to whisper into her ear: "Just want you to know, I like it a bit rough."

"I don't care what you like." She grabbed a dog collar hanging from the ceiling and placed it around Sebastian's neck, pulling down on the chain. "You will like what I tell you to like."

The dominatrix immediately let go of the chain and walked over to a wooden armoire at the back of the cell. She opened the doors to reveal a variety of leather whips and tethers for her choosing. Without hesitation, she pulled out the most hardcore device: a large metal flogger with long, rusted chain-link straps.

Sebastian remained helpless, chained to the wall.

"Don't you need my safe word?"

Silence.

"Oh, and please be careful with whatever you're using 'cause the last time I was here, I had a helluva time explaining the— "

WHAAAP!!!

"—marks to my wife."

Sebastian's eyes screamed pure ecstasy.

"Shut the fuck up. I don't want to hear you talk. I only want to hear you *beg*."

"What should I beg for?"

She moved in close behind him and grabbed his waist tightly. "Me." She licked the base of his neck, rubbing the handle of the whip against his thigh, moving it towards his groin.

Sebastian leaned backwards to whisper again, knowing quite well the walls enjoyed listening. "Let me fuck you. I'll pay you whatever you want."

The dominatrix stepped back.

WHAAAP!!!

Sebastian savored the moment.

She moved back in and continued to fondle him. "Then say my name, you worthless piece of shit."

Wait.

Sebastian hesitated for a moment then cracked a smile. He screwed up the game.

"I'm sorry. I totally forgot your name."

The dominatrix yanked his dog collar chain, jerking his head violently.

"What. Is. My. Name?"

Within seconds, Sebastian felt great pressure against his larynx. "Forgive me…my memory sucks…too many drugs in college."

The dominatrix let go of the chain and returned to the back of the cell.

Sebastian coughed as he recovered, unable to see what she was doing. "You're a serious one, aren't you?"

She opened the armoire doors, removed her biker cap and placed it over the security camera sitting directly behind the ornate keyhole.

"If you tell me your name again, I promise I won't forget it," he pleaded, still facing the dark concrete wall before him.

Silence.

"Are you still here?"

Suddenly, the dominatrix SPRUNG behind him, covered his mouth with a wide black strap and tied it tightly behind his head. "No more talking."

She then unlocked his right hand from the cuff, manually guiding his masturbation. "You forgot my name, fat boy, didn't you?"

Sebastian nodded his head gently, now completely focused on the act of self-pleasure. *Man, this woman is good.*

The dominatrix slowly pulled her hand out of his boxer shorts…

Raised her painted red lips to his ear…

And spoke without her well-rehearsed Russian accent: "I bet you do remember my name, Sebastian."

Wait, how does she…?

"It's Ava."

That voice.

"Ava DeSantis."

Impossible.

His pale blue eyes filled with surprise as she hurled a thick, clear plastic bag over his head…twisting and twisting and twisting the bottom of the bag clenched tightly in her grip.

"MMMHHUUR!!! MMMHHUUR!!!"

"Good to see you again."

"MMMHHUUR!!! MMMHHUUR!!!"

"Looks like you put on a little weight though. Not surprising."

Sebastian struggled to breathe for no less than three minutes…gulping air like a dying fish with soul-less eyes...until finally, his breath slowed with resolution that this was indeed his final moment.

Let me live, Ava. I can make things right.

But no words came out of his mouth...only his eyes spoke through the foggy bag...until those pale blue fish eyes filled with the glorious sound of silence.

CHAPTER 2

"WHO THE FUCK IS AVA DESANTIS?"

FRIDAY, JANUARY 25, 1991
1:32 P.M.

Twenty-one-year-old Sebastian O'Connor stood like a river boulder in a stream of college students, reading aloud from a test results chart posted on a classroom door.

"No really, who the fuck *is* that?"

His best friend smiled and pointed to a plain girl in grunge clothing standing directly behind Sebastian. It was (you guessed it) eighteen-year-old Ava DeSantis.

Sebastian's best friend, Wesley Scarborough, was a well-bred Southern frat boy who wasn't just handsome, he was A-list *movie star* handsome. He was tall and built with a commanding physique. His light golden was face framed by thick, surfer-blonde hair, long enough to cover his ears and kiss his enviable eyelashes. His strong, perfectly chiseled chin upstaged only by a pair of cerulean blue eyes made famous by the Viking clans of his ancestral home of Yorkshire, England.

But what made Wesley an instant celebrity on campus weren't his good looks, his famous father or his famous last name. It was his *smile*. A smile so authentic and disarming that it could peel the sweatpants off a gold star lesbian from ten feet away.

Ava on the other hand was the complete opposite of Wesley, a perfect contradiction to the herds of beauty pageant girls attending this small, prestigious university. She was tall and lanky with light olive skin, large moss-green eyes and straight-as-glass dark reddish-brown hair. She lacked any sense of modern style, dressing like a homeless librarian at a school where the term "label whore" was a compliment.

She most certainly favored her deceased, mild-mannered (but tough-as-nails) Irish mother so much more than her dark, hot-tempered Greek father. She even inherited her mother's Gaelic gaze: a casual, harmless, hypnotic stare that could send Steven King-style spine-chills without any maleficence behind it.

Despite all of this, it was actually Ava's *voice* that gave away her biggest social problem. Deep and disheveled, one knew in five seconds that Atlanta was not her native ground.

Sebastian awkwardly turned to acknowledge her standing behind him.

"Hey."

Ava said nothing. Instead she pulled up the hood of her brown sweatshirt, shrank away from the crowd and headed towards the exit.

Sebastian rolled his eyes as she left. "What a freak."

Wesley cocked his chiseled chin. "I thought Zindler didn't give out A's?"

"That's what I heard."

Wesley looked over to the door where Ava exited and immediately followed her outside.

During the winter months, the campus of Anniston University had a Brothers Grimm fairytale feel to it. The main courtyard was vast and comprised of dead grass and barren trees surrounded by castle-like buildings made of varying shades of silver stone. Students were sparse, given the weather was cold for Atlanta, although most Northerners would deem it mild, considering it was the dead middle of winter. The slate gray sky watched over

Ava as she walked with purpose down a straight concrete path that emptied into a packed parking lot in the distance.

"Hey, Ava!" yelled Wesley from five yards behind. "Excuse me, Ava!"

She stopped and turned around.

"Your name is Ava, right?"

She nodded.

"Well, congratulations."

"For what?" she said shyly in her native New Jersey accent.

"For getting the highest score on Zindler's test. No one else even came close."

"Oh. Thank you."

Ava resumed walking. Wesley continued to follow.

"I'm sorry. I don't think we've been properly introduced. I'm Wesley Scar—"

"I know who you are."

He flashed that million-dollar smile. "I guess I overdid it with the campaign posters."

"I'm sorry, I didn't vote."

They continued walking towards the slush-filled parking lot a hundred yards away. Silence brewed between them.

"Am I…is this a bad time?"

"I'm late for work."

"I can see that." Wesley carefully stepped over a pile of dog shit. "I'm just real curious about something, Ava. How did you get an A on that test?"

"What do you mean?"

"I mean, how did you do so well?"

She stopped, hand on hip. "I studied." At that moment, she launched her hypnotic gaze, head titled at an angle that seemed almost offensive.

"Well, I studied too and got a D." Wesley was equally steadfast, not lowering a single eyelash to combat her formidable stare.

After a few long seconds, Ava broke the connection. "I'm sorry. I've really got to run."

She hastened her pace until she broke free from Wesley, heart-beating, feeling as if she was under interrogation. *Why is he talking to me?* She was a second semester freshman. A real nobody. No one at school ever spoke to her, except for the fat Mormon girl at the end of her dorm hallway who tried to befriend every living creature. *What could Wesley Scarborough possibly want with me?*

Just as Ava was thinking this, he began yelling from behind her.

"There's rumors floatin' around that Zindler gets graduate students to create tests for him. And sometimes those grad students have friends, female friends. Know what I mean?"

Ava continued without breaking stride, "No. Sorry, I don't!"

Wesley quickly realized that a city-girl smart enough to coax the test answers out of a graduate student was surely too smart to reveal her sources up front. So, in perfect Southern fashion, he turned the Scarborough charm-laser on full blast.

"Wait!" he hollered, vigorously jogging to catch up to her. "This is coming out all wrong."

Ava hesitated at first then gave him her full attention. "What do you whaant with me?"

(My ears! That grating accent!)

"I just wanted to ask you, nicely of course, if you would consider tutoring me. Like a part-time job or something."

"I already have a job." She fought an impending yawn. "What I need is sleep."

"But what if I paid you *twice* what you're making now?"

Ava reacted. "Excuse me?"

"Whatever it is, I'll pay it."

Her expression said: *you must be crazy.*

"I mean, how much do you make a week? A thousand? Two thousand?"

Now she *knew* he was crazy. "Try two hundred."

"Okay. Double that."

What? Ava was even more suspicious of his intentions. She had studied just as hard as anyone else for that test and was surprised her classmates didn't find Zindler's questions one hundred percent predictable. However, unlike her peers, she had already read at least fifteen books on World War II prior to even stepping foot in his *History of the Third Reich* class.

Unbeknownst to her, most of Ava's privileged classmates treated reading as a forced-at-gunpoint-activity... like dying, voting liberal or paying taxes.

"What would I have to do exactly?" she asked.

"I don't know. Just come by my house a couple of times a week and help me study."

Ava was doubtful.

"You know, just tutor me. Tutor me in this boring Hitler shit."

Ava recoiled for a moment. "So you're willing to *pay me* four hundred bucks a week?"

"Yes."

"To come by your house?"

"Yes."

"And help you study?"

"Yes."

"That's it?"

"Yes!" Wesley smiled.

Holy shit dude, how rich are you?

Ava's father had grown up poor in a tough section of Astoria, Queens, which prepared him well for his career in the Atlantic City gaming industry where he'd been working for the past thirty years. Among the many life lessons she sadly had to learn as a young girl, her father often warned her, *Easy money always comes with a big price tag.*

"Thanks for the offer, but I'll pass."

Wesley was visibly shocked by her answer. He drew a deep breath, and then launched his final missile. "Look, I want to be totally honest with you. But I need to know this will stay between us," he said in a mature and formal tone.

"Okay."

"No, I'm serious as a dead skunk."

"Don't worry. No one here even speaks to me anyways."

Wesley looked around the courtyard to see if anyone was close enough to listen. He leaned in, grabbed Ava by the shoulders, and whispered inches from the tip of her long, classical nose. "Ava, this is my second time taking Zindler's class. If I don't get at least a B this time, I won't graduate this spring. And if I don't graduate this spring, I won't get into law school next year. And if I don't get into law school next year, my father's going to hang me up by my big toes, buck naked in our front yard, for the entire neighborhood to see!"

Wesley erupted into juvenile laugher.

Ava was oddly charmed by his corny Southern humor. *Beneath all this hunkiness, he's just a dork like me*, she thought.

"You'd be preventing a murder, Ava! Now, how can you deny me knowing my grave situation?" He once again flashed that million-dollar smile (felt miles away by females everywhere).

Ava returned a half-assed smile. *Maybe this isn't so bad*, she thought. *Maybe he's just some rich kid willing to pay anything to pass this class.*

"Come on, Ava. What do you say?"

Four hundred dollars. Crazy money! But my God…

"Okay, I'll think about it," she said in a turn of heart.

"Great! Perfect."

Still walking in tandem, they finally arrived at her car. It was a yellow, rusted out '79 Camaro, drowning in a sea of luxury vehicles.

"You know, why don't you come by the Zeta House tonight? We're having a party to celebrate Hussein getting his ass kicked. We can finalize the details there."

"But I thought only sorority girls could get into frat parties?"

"That would be true if you weren't my special guest. Here," Wesley pulled out a felt-tip pen from his leather bomber jacket, grabbed Ava's hand and signed *Wesley Scarborough* above her knuckles. "Now, don't wash that off. Show it to the guy at the front door and everything should be fine."

"Which house is it?"

Wesley gleamed. He'd won her over. "It's the second one on the right. Zeta Omega. You can't miss it."

Ava entered her car, shivering in the cold, black seat as she placed the key into the ignition and started it. The parking lot rumbled with the sound of her rusty, badass Camaro.

"Come by around ten!" shouted Wesley.

Ava's car raced even louder as she pulled out of the parking spot. She rolled down the window, struggling to speak over the thunderous noise. "I get off of work at eleven!"

"Come by after work then! And don't forget to tell your boss that you quit!"

Ava smiled wide as she drove off. Tickled to death to quit her shitty waitress job and make kick-ass money tutoring the hottest guy on campus.

Yeah. Life. Is. Awesome.

Wesley waved good-bye as he watched her leave the parking lot and turn onto a busy street. Suddenly, Sebastian popped up right beside him.

"Hey, what was that all about?"

"I invited her to the house tonight."

"What the hell you do that for? She's a goddamn freak."

"Because she's got Zindler's tests, *that's* why."

"She told you that?"

"No, she's not admitting anything yet. But I'm going to get my hands on those fucking tests. You watch and see."

"Cool." Sebastian slapped Wesley on the back. "Just be willing to share, good buddy."

CHAPTER 3

THE SPERM LOTTERY

FRIDAY, JANUARY 25, 1991
11:55 P.M.

The temple of the Zeta Omega House was exactly what one would expect from a wealthy fraternal organization: a twelve thousand-square-foot, brick antebellum home with a white wrap-around porch and gleaming gold *Zeta* and *Omega* letters prominently displayed above the row of windows on the second floor. Instead of showcasing condoms and beer cans and other pre-pubescent litter of cinema folklore, the Zeta Omega House was freshly painted, exquisitely landscaped and always spotless – as in *all-ways*.

During the warmer months, the house was adorned with the fraternal order's colors of red and white: specifically, beautiful white magnolia tree blossoms in the yard and red hibiscus plants along the front walkway. The perpetually green lawn was made of AstroTurf and the perfectly manicured plants along the porch were made of the finest Chinese silk and perfect for winter. A dozen large wooden rocking chairs lined the porch, but that evening was one of the coldest of the season, keeping the majority of its fragile residents warmly inside.

Ava approached the elevated doorstep of the house wearing a candy-pink, fifties diner waitress uniform and a worn-out (but incredibly warm) yellow wool coat. Her hair was styled high in a girlish ponytail, completing the pompom girl persona she was forced to present to annoying tourists every night. She had serendipitously found a parking spot very close to the main entrance, and walked back to her car two times before getting the courage to knock on the huge coffin, plantation-style front door.

Ava knocked.

She knocked again harder.

She could clearly hear the muffled sound of music coming from inside but wasn't sure if anyone could hear her. *This must be a sign*, she thought. *I should go*. Ava huffed in disappointment, but quickly gathered the courage to try one last time. She took several steps to the left to peer through the window closest to the front door. She knocked on the glass. Shadows of co-eds stood motionless on the other side. *Come on guys, see me.* A tall man inside the house finally acknowledged her and gestured to come back around to the front door.

Damn. Finally. The door opened. The frat boy behind it was impeccably dressed, but so tall and redneck that he looked like the host of *Trailer Park Masterpiece Theatre.* "The infirmary is across the street," he snuffed, and then attempted to close the door in haste.

Ava put out her hand out to stop him. "Wesley Scarborough invited me."

He scrutinized her closely. "You must be confusing our Wesley with someone else."

Ava immediately showed him the signature on her hand.

Redneck Lurch cocked his eyes, begrudgingly letting her in without saying a word.

Inside, Ava took off her worn-out yellow coat and tossed it to him. "Careful," she said, mocking his pretentious tone. "It's an heirloom."

———— ❧ ————

The interior of Zeta Omega was surprising sophisticated. Wood paneling, brown leather sofas and exotic hardwood floors made it perfectly clear that these kids had hit the sperm lottery. With jazz music playing softly in the background, Ava self-consciously looked around the crowded room to see if she could find anyone she knew.

Meanwhile, Sebastian (wearing a navy blazer with a red bow tie) and Wesley (wearing a blue, long-sleeved polo shirt, collar up) stood at the back of the grand ballroom, unable to see her enter. Both were heavily into their discussion with dark colored cocktails in hand.

"Nope. I don't wait for anyone. Let's go."

"Just give her five more minutes."

"She ain't showing up, Wes! It's midnight. Let's go."

Just then, their third-wheel-friend, David Reilly returned from the kitchen holding an overflowing glass of Scotch. He was below average intelligence, and *way* below average looking, with troubled skin, light brown hair and dark narrow eyes. He stood only about five-feet-seven, and was so jittery and hyper that he could make a person tired just by looking at him.

"There's not a goddamn drop of Scotch left in this entire place," said David. "I looked everywhere. Nothing."

"What about the CDs?" asked Wesley.

"Now *those* I did find. Got one for each of us." He gestured to the breast pocket of his plaid dinner jacket that was way too small to hold three compact discs. "And these were Beau's very last ones, so let's get out of here."

"Wesley wants to wait for that possessed girl," griped Sebastian.

"She's not possessed."

"Looks like a green-pea-soup-spitter to me." Sebastian smugly sipped his cocktail.

"Who the hell's that?"

"Oh great, there she is," said Wesley as he watched Ava squirm through the crowd of trust-fund babies. "Hey, Ava! Over here!"

"Ladies and gentleman, it is my absolute pleasure to present…Wesley's latest charity case!" mocked Sebastian.

"I'm sorry I'm late. Things were really crazy tonight," she said panting, missing Sebastian's comment by a nanosecond.

"No problem. We're just glad you made it," replied Wesley. "You've already met my esteemed colleague, Sebastian O'Connor, right?"

"Not formally."

Sebastian pointed to her waitress nametag. "Love their milkshakes."

"Oh, thanks, I forgot about that." She quickly removed her nametag while Sebastian glared at her, completely appalled with what she was wearing.

"And this is our third partner-in-crime, David Reilly," continued Wesley.

"I've heard a lot about Ava lately. It's nice to finally meet you," he slurred.

"Same here…Cool, uh, where can I grab a beer?" she asked.

"Beer? Let's see, maybe there's some in the basement. I'll go check for you," raved Wesley. "Don't go anywhere, promise?"

"Don't worry, I won't," she smiled back.

At that very moment, Sebastian caught a whiff of genuine chemistry between them. Needless to say he was *not pleased*. Why? Because despite having a steady, blueblood girlfriend at another school, Wesley had a nasty habit of bringing single-serve locals into their exclusive events. Good-looking, big-titted, working class girls who were just there to hog up the booze and hoover up their coke, the two commodities Sebastian treasured most at that age. Ava may not have been a local, but she was definitely unattractive and poor, and worse yet, she was unimportant...the *ultimate* turn off in Sebastian's playbook.

For one long, awkward minute, Ava stood in silence with Sebastian and David, straining for something to say. Finally, she came up with some small talk.

"This place is absolutely gorgeous. You guys are so friggin' lucky."

"Should be. We pay a shitload in dues," snapped Sebastian.

She spotted a state-of-the-art projection screen television at the opposite end of the room. There was no sound, only the images of planes bombing Iraq and the perpetually gray-haired Wolf Blitzer reporting. "So, do you guys think this is going to be the next Vietnam? This whole war thing is pretty scary."

"No. We'll win this one," replied Sebastian.

"Really?"

"No doubt about it."

"How can you be so sure?"

"I don't think American citizens should question the capabilities of our military."

"I'm not questioning our military's *capabilities*, I just don't think this war's in the bag like Bush does," said Ava.

"Oh, shit," whispered David under his breath.

A blue vein popped in between Sebastian's invisible eyebrows. "George Herbert Walker Bush personally flew fifty-eight combat missions until he was shot down by the goddamn Japs in World War II. He received a fucking medal for *bravery in action*. Plus, my grandfather plays golf with him at least once a year in Kennebunkport. I think our president knows what he's doing."

"Let me guess…you're a Democrat."

Sebastian's pale blue eyes lit on fire while David chuckled at her ballsy comment.

"We're not talking politics, kids, are we?" Wesley arrived just in time and handed Ava a bottle of imported beer from Switzerland.

"Thanks."

"So how was work tonight?"

"It sucked. We were three girls short. That's why I was so late. Again, I am so sorry."

"Well, that'll all be over with soon, right?"

"Well, that's why I'm here," she smiled.

Sebastian was now at his breaking point. His cheeks were full, filled with blood like an albino rhino ready to charge. "I'm ready to go home, y'all. Let's fucking *go*."

"Now hold on, Sebastian, Ava just got here."

"Let's fucking go."

"Ava, would you care to join us for cocktails at our place?"

Sebastian shot Wesley a look of imminent death.

"Wait, I thought you guys lived *here*?"

"We *did*, but Wesley got a house for his birthday," chimed David.

"Wow. Okay, sure. Why not?"

Sebastian visibly festered in silence.

"Do you need to get up early tomorrow morning or something? Are you cool to stay out tonight?" asked Wesley.

"Actually Saturday is my only day to sleep in. I close Saturday nights."

"Perfect. Time to party then." Wesley patted his pants for keys.

Sebastian took the glass of Scotch out of David's hand and offered it to Ava. "Here. Drink up."

"What is it?"

"It's the house wine of the South. You need to catch up."

"Thanks, but I can't handle liquor very well."

Sebastian pinned her down to the mat of college peer pressure. "I'm surprised. I heard Yankee girls were way tougher than that."

David lightly gasped.

Ava winced at the smell of the Scotch, then met Sebastian's stare with equal vigor. She took the full glass out of his hand and slammed the whole thing in one shot.

"Whoa!" said David.

"Alrighty then," said Wesley. "Time to go."

"Did you drive here, Ava?" asked David.

"Yes," she said, still choking from the single-malt burn in her throat.

"Good, you can follow me then."

"Okay…Just don't drive too fast."

CHAPTER 4

BLACK ACRE

SATURDAY, JANUARY 26, 1991
1:23 A.M.

Wesley parked – no, slammed – his brand new, black 1991 BMW 525i onto the curb directly in front of a dilapidated, two-story antebellum home. "Fuck you!" he said as he swung open the driver's side door.

"Admit it. I can see it in your eyes," said Sebastian, exiting the passenger side.

"But can you see it in his pants?" blurted David, falling out of the back seat and onto the ground. Wesley curled his face in annoyance. Sebastian shrugged the shoulder tabs of his Burberry trench coat as if to say, *the boy's got a point.*

Just then, Ava's loud, yellow Camaro pulled around the corner and drove directly towards Wesley's parked car. Sebastian walked into the middle of the empty street. His strawberry blonde hair nearly disappeared in the spotlight of Ava's approaching headlights. "You owe me, Wes," he said in a solemn tone. "*Big* time."

⁕

The three co-eds swayed on the porch, freezing and dancing and freezing some more while Wesley fumbled inside his leather bomber jacket to find his keys. To keep her mind off the cold, Ava turned her attention to the outside of Wesley's home. Quietly, she was shocked anyone would want to live there. Yes, the home was huge and beautiful and in the historic neighborhood of Ansley Park, but its dingy white façade and peeling black plantation shutters made it look like the perfect place to shoot a low-budget horror film. Even the four white Corinthian columns guarding the entrance were now dark green, covered by the oppressive vines that had strangled them years ago. *Spooky house*, she thought to herself. *Thank God I am not alone.*

"Shit, I forgot my coat," she said out loud, shivering in the early morning darkness.

"Not to worry. It'll be safe at Zeta House," slurred David.

"Come on, fucker, it's colder than a witch's tit in a brass bra!" yelled Sebastian just as Wesley tugged the key out of his left pant pocket. Seconds later, an eighty-year-old, blue-haired woman in a flannel nightgown burst onto her large porch next door.

"Sorry, Mrs. Lipton. We'll keep it down," said Wesley.

Mrs. Lipton scowled back at him. She then reached into her flannel pocket, pulled out two neon pink earplugs and forcefully shoved them one by one into each ear. Sebastian innocently smiled and waved back to her, while David and Ava stared humbly at the floor.

Mrs. Lipton turned away, flipped them the bird and walked back inside.

Wesley finally opened the door. "Welcome to *Black Acre!*"

Ava was eager to step through the threshold into the warmth, but was immediately taken aback by what she saw. The interior of the house was structurally beautiful but a total shitfest of a mess inside. Patio furniture occupied the living room. Pizza boxes and clothing were scattered everywhere. There was no doubt in her mind that three spoiled slobs occupied this over-the-top bachelor pad.

"Please excuse the pigsty," said Wesley.

"The maid got deported," added David.

"Wow. This place is amazing." Ava hopped over several small piles of dirty clothing on her way the center of the wood-floored living room. In awe, she twirled around like Marlo Thomas in *That Girl*. "I can't believe you guys actually live here." She then proceeded to walk over to one of the walls, touching the hand painted parchment finish. "When was it built?"

"Eighteen-fifty, I think. It's been in my mother's family for over a century," said Wesley.

"Wow."

Ava looked at the dark oak double staircase leading up to the second floor. Several spindles were missing or broken on the railing. "What's upstairs?"

"We don't know," replied David.

"You don't know?"

"We don't go upstairs," chimed Sebastian.

"May I ask why?" Ava directed her question to Sebastian. Wesley listened intently as he hung up his jacket in the front closet, waiting to hear Sebastian's response.

"There's a local tale that the second floor of this home is haunted...haunted by Wesley's Bible-thumping great aunt who use to live here with eighty some cats."

"Sometimes you can still smell *cat stench* when it's real quiet," added David.

"Story was that the old lady was so fucking crazy and so damn religious that she believed the Devil was making her cats multiply. At night, she would take the pregnant cats and tie their legs together with rope so they couldn't give birth...until all of the female cats in the house died. Then, one night, when she wasn't expecting it, the male cats got real lonely. They crawled into her bed...went under the sheets...up her legs..."

"And ate her pussy!" babbled David.

Wesley burst out laughing. "Y'all are so full of shit! *They* sleep upstairs."

"Oh, good," she said, visibly relieved. "I'm not really a big fan of cats."

Now *that* was an understatement. For years, Ava absolutely *hated* cats. In fact, it was a cat who had run across the road on a warm summer evening in 1982, when her mother, driving home from the grocery store, swerved to avoid hitting it and lost control of the car, running head first into a telephone pole.

Just like that. Cat. Mother. Dead.

"Let's get some booze, y'all" barked Sebastian as he threw his trench coat to the floor and walked over to a shiny teak bar at the back of the living room.

Ava caught herself zoning out about how much she missed her foul-mouthed mother. "Uh, no more alcohol for me, guys. I have to drive home tonight." She then glided over to a white and green striped plastic chair located dangerously near the fireplace.

She sat down and started to bounce. "Is this patio—?"

"Funny how the heir to the furniture dynasty has no goddamn furniture," joked Sebastian.

"*Scarborough* furniture?" asked Ava.

"Now you're really starting to sound like my daddy, Sebastian."

"No friggin' way, that's *you*?" asked Ava once again, finally understanding why so many girls wanted to get their MRS degree with Wesley. "I had no idea, I didn't realize… Wow. You have like stores everywhere." As she was speaking, Sebastian handed her a dirty glass full of Scotch.

"Actually, my grandfather started the company," replied Wesley.

Ava downed the shot. "Then why are you so worried about getting into law school?" she coughed.

"'Cause daddy's a judge," interrupted David.

"No, it's because Wes is a momma's boy," added Sebastian.

"What he *means* to say is that my mother is a lawyer."

"Not just any lawyer. She's a badass bitch with a briefcase," said Sebastian.

"Now ain't that *your* type?" joked David.

Sebastian flipped him the bird.

"Wow, I'm impressed," said Ava. "What kind of law does she practice?"

"Criminal defense," replied Wesley.

"And your father's a judge?"

"Yep. That's how they met. She was defending the Richard Crown death penalty case and he was on the bench. I guess, somehow, through all those crime scene photos of blown out nun brains, they fell in love."

"Romantic."

"Love at first sight, I'm sure," snarled Sebastian.

Wesley headed toward the bar to pour himself a cocktail. "Need something to drink, sweetie? Jack and Coke sound good?"

Sebastian's eyes darkened. *Sweetie?*

"No, I'm good for now, thanks."

"So where you from, Ava?" asked David.

"Atlantic City."

"New Jersey?'

"No, Mississippi you dumb ass. Damn, you're stupid," said Wesley.

"Ahhh, yes. Atlantic City. The land of Donald Trump, fixed tables and cheap hookers," added Sebastian.

Wesley moved closer to Ava and leaned into her ear. "Do you mind if we go into my room to talk business for a while?"

Sebastian noticed.

"Of course not. That's why I'm here, right?"

Wesley turned to address the others. "Gentlemen, please excuse us." He gently gripped Ava's hand, lifted her from the patio chair and led her down the dark hallway.

"So, Ava, do you charge by the hour or by the night?" whispered David as he slumped over the outdoor patio sofa laughing.

Oh my God, we aren't going to have sex, are we?

Ava was totally unprepared for this moment. She was quite drunk, heart fluttering, completely stunned to be in Wesley Scarborough's bedroom *(internal sigh)*. Without sobriety holding her together, she experienced her emotions full force: *He's gorgeous*, she thought. *But I have no underwear on…I forgot to shave my legs…I should have showered after work…*she repeated over and over. But then the real zinger: *God help me, I don't even know how to do it. What the hell am I doing here?*

Although not a virgin, Ava had only had sex twice before with the comic book nerd across the street from her home in New Jersey. It wasn't even sex really, just a mutual agreement to a few seconds of intercourse so they wouldn't die virgins in a car wreck or zombie apocalypse. The whole experience was awful for the both of them, but in her mind, completely necessary. *That didn't count*, she thought. In her mind, she was still technically a virgin, saving herself for the first man to fall in love with her. Maybe that man would be Wesley. And maybe that first time would be tonight.

—⊶⊷—

Wesley's bedroom looked like a rock star's sanctuary. It was an unusually large place with a gargantuan Kenwood stereo system at one end, and a California king-size waterbed, television, dresser and overstuffed red chair at the other. Unlike the rest of the home, Wesley's bedroom was pristine and tidy. The dark wood floor cradled an elegant Asian throw rug, and the sparkling white walls were adorned with thick gold-framed autographed album covers from the Kings of Southern Rock: The Allman Brothers Band, The Georgia Satellites, The Black Crowes, The Outlaws, The Marshall Tucker Band, The Kentucky Headhunters, Molly Hatchet, Charlie Daniels, ZZ Top and three from Lynyrd Skynyrd, Wesley's all time favorite band *of all time*. Even the bed was made up perfectly with a black and gold jacquard comforter, crushed by oversized fringed *manly* decorative pillows.

This place is awesome, Ava concluded.

"Sit down," said Wesley as he patted the top of his waterbed. "It's motionless."

Ava smiled as she plunged down into the bed.

"See, I told you. Comfy."

She beamed, drunk as a skunk. "So, uh, where do we start? I'm not sure how—"

Wesley interrupted. "Why Anniston University? It's a million miles away from Atlantic City."

"Oh, uh, it was the only school that gave me a full scholarship. I was accepted to Princeton, but tuition there for a month was more than my dad made in a year."

"I see."

"Plus, I heard Southerners were really nice people." Ava cracked an awkward smile.

"Well, we are." He softly moved a dark brown tendril hanging from her ponytail. "The girls here. They're rough on you, aren't they?"

"They can be," she admitted reluctantly.

Wesley looked into Ava's large, woodsy-green eyes, and saw something he hadn't noticed before: *a gentle soul.* A soul that was oddly fragile yet iron-forged at the same time. A soul who wouldn't judge or criticize a person but instead would be willing to give her last dollar to a homeless man by the side of the road. In some strange way, Wesley found this quality in Ava very appealing. In fact, it made her *beautiful.* And where she lacked in physical attractiveness, she made up for in radiant gentleness. And despite being as intoxicated as he was, Wesley soon abandoned his Zindler test-seeking mission and began to feel genuine feelings for her. See, Ava was unlike any other girl in this town. She was smart. She was down-to-earth. And in a super-human kind of way, extremely kind. And maybe she was a girl whom, for once in Wesley's life, he could take seriously.

Ava noticed a picture on his dresser. It was an 8x10 photograph of a bikini-clad blonde holding up a big mouth bass on a boat.

"Is that your girlfriend?"

"Yeah. That's Emma. She goes to Margaret Scott. Daddy made her go to an all-girl school because Anniston is too wild for his little darlin'."

"Do you see her much?"

Wesley paused then shrugged his shoulders. "She gives me my space."

Ava inspected the photo closely. "She's *beautiful*."

Wesley's deep blue eyes looked through Ava in a way that said: *so are you.* Ava turned to look back at him, feeling every ounce of the infatuation he was feeling. Her gaze now flowed a stream of warmth that spoke volumes of how she could one day *love* him. Love him unconditionally. Without judgment. Or expectations. Or criticism.

Wesley leaned in closer and began to kiss her. First, softy on the lips, and then, for a few special moments, he opened his mouth wide and merged his tongue with hers, making love to her before even one piece of clothing was removed…Then, just as Wesley lifted his hand to place it on Ava's beating breast, Sebastian and David barged through the bedroom door.

"I thought we had a party going on here?" yelled Sebastian.

"What the fuck are—?" squealed Wesley.

"Hey, Ava, you wanna get high with us?" asked David.

"Uh, I don't smoke pot, really."

"Oh, we *ain't* talking weed, little girl," said Sebastian as he offered Ava another glass of Scotch. She shook her head. He kept his arm out. Finally, she grabbed the glass and sipped it.

"Come on, man!" Wesley was now annoyed beyond measure. "Give me a fucking break."

"What? We were just getting to know our new house guest and you took her away from us." Sebastian plopped his fat ass into the overstuffed red chair.

At the same time, David rifled through Wesley's top dresser drawer. He pulled out a pink sock, then a white bow tie, and then a small black .22 caliber pistol. He inspected it closely. "Ain't this a bitch gun?"

"Put that shit down!" hollered Wesley.

David quickly placed the gun back into the drawer and closed it.

"Before we were so rudely interrupted, Ava" Sebastian glared over to Wesley. "You were telling us about yourself. What does your father do for a living?"

"He's a black jack dealer. In a casino."

"And mother?"

"She died in a car accident when I was nine."

David reacted. "That sucks."

Wesley looked at both of his roommates in amazement.

"Got any brothers or sisters?" asked Sebastian.

"No. My mom had a—"

"Is this fucking twenty questions?" yelled Wesley.

"Chill out, Wes. We're just trying to get to know our new friend." Sebastian immediately returned to interrogating Ava. "Your mom had what?"

"She had a hard time getting pregnant with me. Which is why, when I was little, she would always say that she hoped I'd give her ten grandkids one day."

"Ten? That's a wetback litter," slurred David.

"I'm sure she was just exaggerating."

"DeSantis. Now is that name Italian or Porta Ree-can?" Wesley rolled his eyes.

"Uh, no, neither actually. My mother was from Northern Ireland. And my father's parents were from Greece."

"Cool. I never meet a Greek before," added David.

Sitting in his red throne of inquisition, Sebastian leaned into his thigh as if he was about to make a long speech. "Did you know that the word Greek means *slave*?"

"That's enough, Sebastian."

"No really, Wes." Sebastian cocked his head slightly, peering directly into Ava's eyes. "During the eighteenth century, a bunch of French fags overheard the Turks call boys from Hellas *grecs*, which is of course, the Turkish word for slave. Since the French are born with diarrhea of the mouth, they went out and told the whole fucking world what they overheard. So from that point on, a person from Hellas was called a *grec*, which later evolved into the word *Greek*. Greek means slave."

Ava downed the rest of her drink. "Really? And when did the French overhear the word *asshole*?"

"Busted!" blurted David.

"Fuck you," replied Sebastian.

"Where's your bathroom, Wes?"

"Just go straight down the hall. It's the first door on the right."

"Thanks. I'll be right back."

Wesley shot Ava an apologetic look as she left the room. Ava winked back; Sebastian's arrows didn't even make a dent in her armor.

"Well, alrighty then. I'll get some music going."

Ava stood in the hallway with her ear pressed against the closed bedroom door, listening to Wesley and Sebastian fight over her:

"Don't give me that shit! She's cool. And she ain't done a goddamn thing to you."

"Wes, you're wrong."

"Why?"

"She insulted me."

"How?"

"She called me a fucking *Democrat.*"

David laughed.

"And?"

"And? See, David. I told you he was in love."

Ava smiled uncontrollably as she left the door and stumbled down the dark hallway.

Inside the bathroom, she flipped the lights on. *Blinded!* Then once Ava's eyes adjusted, she saw her reflection in the mirror. *Boy, am I wasted.* It was all over her face. Her large eyes were red and droopy, her dark hair was a total mess with strands sticking out in every direction from her failing ponytail. She looked around the large room, impressed with how beautiful it was. The white and gray veined marble floor extended all the way up the walls and into the triple-crown molding holding up a sky-blue painted ceiling. The bathroom fixtures were old, made of brass and covered by antique gold, like something out of a governor's mansion or Civil War museum.

Then it hit her. A wave of nausea that rumbled at first, then poured out of her mouth into the sink. "BLAHHHHHH," she roared as she puked into the white porcelain basin. She turned on the water to rinse her mouth...*Oh, shit.* Again. "BLAHHHHHH," into the tiny white bowl of relief beneath her.

As she raised up, she saw a small piece of vomit on the corner of her mouth. *Now that's sexy.* She was right, she never looked worse in her life. She rinsed again. Still the taste of acid Scotch remained. She looked around the counter to see if there was anything that could help: mouthwash, lip balm, anything. But all she saw was a collection of twenty different bottles of male cologne: Drakkar, Polo, Joop! The brands the popular boys always seemed to wear. *Oh, screw it,* she thought. At least now with her insides empty she felt a million times better.

Ava walked across the long room to the toilet. She placed the seat down (stupid boys) then noticed there was no toilet paper. *Shit.* She spotted a linen closet on the other side of the room. She took three steps before slipping on an invisible puddle from the adjacent shower. *Dammit!* Lucky to not have hit the floor, she realized she was still drunker than she'd ever been in her life. *Get it together, dammit. You can't look this bad in front of Wesley.*

Seconds later, she rummaged through the linen closet: *toilet paper…toilet paper…Oh, here we go.* As she reached for the last roll, she noticed a stack of magazines. She pulled one off the top and saw it was an S&M porn magazine with a leathered-up redhead on the cover. She immediately flipped through the pages, giggling to herself, experiencing a variety of emotions from curiosity to disgust to arousal. *People are sick*, she thought. She then returned the magazine to the secret stash and grabbed the treasured last roll of toilet paper.

———— ❦ ————

Ava staggered toward Wesley's bedroom, now concentrating exclusively on walking forward. *Step by step*, she thought to herself. *One foot goes in front of the other.* As she approached the door, she smelled something strange.

Something toxic. A cross between burning tires and hot bleach. *What is that smell?* As she came closer, she heard the distinctive sounds of boiling water and a woman moaning. Once again, she pressed her ear up to the door and listened closely:

"Are you sure Beau said to mix this with Angel?" asked Wesley.

"Best trip he ever had," replied David.

"Fuck, man. Why are we watching this shit?"

"Cause I like dark meat," replied Sebastian.

"Just hit it, Wes! Stop hogging it up," said David.

Ava hesitated outside the door. She instantly felt a ten-pound knot grow in her stomach, but didn't know why. *I should go home.* But as soon as the thought crossed her mind, she remembered how impossible it would be to drive thirty-five minutes up I-285 given her intoxicated state. *Wait, I can just crash on the couch. But wait, hell no, this place is haunted. Shit. Maybe Wesley will have a better idea. Maybe I can crash in his room. Yes, that's it.*

Ava opened the door and entered slowly. As she stepped inside, she saw the television playing a video of two old white men having sex with a young black woman; the unhappy girl in the middle giving a blowjob to the wrinkled bald man in front while getting screwed by the gray-haired fat man behind her. Ava also spotted Sebastian and David, with bloodshot red eyes, silently staring at the video like cats watching canaries. But what was *most* disturbing was seeing her dear Prince Charming Wesley, sitting on the bed all alone, sweating profusely...

Smoking crack.

Ava was confused. "Hey guys, I'm going to take off. I just remembered that I have to take this girl's shift tomorrow morning."

"Why the huge rush?" asked Sebastian. "You should stay a while."

Ava hesitated. "Um, okay, but like only for a minute, then I need to go." As she spoke, David walked behind her and quietly locked the bedroom door.

"Where's that music, maestro? Move it!" commanded Sebastian.

Wesley, still finishing up his hit, continued sucking the clear glass tube attached to a tar stained bulb. He held his breath for a few moments then coughed a cloud of dingy gray smoke out of his body. His beautiful sun-kissed blonde hair was now greasy and sweaty, tainted by the chemical burning smell lurching in the room. "Cut that shit off," he said to Sebastian. "There's a lady present in the room."

"Why? Ava doesn't mind." Sebastian's eyes were as black as coal. "Do you, Ava?"

Ava was stunned. She didn't know how to answer. Despite being from a rough neighborhood in Atlantic City, she had never even seen crack before let alone been around people who smoked it. She was a Nancy Reagan child of the eighties after all. Just say no. *Just say no.*

Meanwhile, Wesley walked over to David who was now jittery beyond words, leaning heavily against the dresser. Wesley handed him the hot glass pipe.

"Why, thank you," he said as he searched his breast pocket for the last rock.

"Music. Coming right up." Wesley continued walking to the far end of the room, completely unaware of what the others were doing behind him. Once he arrived, he turned all of his attention to his beloved Kenwood stereo. *What a beast* he thought. He lightly touched the imported wood cabinet, moving his fingers gently across the top and then down to the POWER button on the receiver. He pushed it. Lights flared everywhere. As he moved his eyes, the neon green stereo lights created tracers, tracers that danced in a synchronized pattern like primitive tribesmen performing for their ancient alien masters.

Wesley picked up a cassette box from a stack of tapes piled on the speaker. On the white lined cover it read: *For My Wesley, Love Emma* in purple handwriting. It was a delicious mix tape Wesley's girlfriend had made of all of his favorite songs for his birthday. *I wish I could get this on CD*, he thought. But for now, cassette tape will do.

His finger moved down the system to the tape deck. Wesley pressed OPEN. He slipped the cassette inside and pressed PLAY. After a few blank seconds, the guitar rift intro for Lynyrd Skynyrd's *Simple Man* blasted through the five-foot speakers. *God I love this song*, he thought to himself. Heaven. *Pure Heaven.*

As the music played, Wesley felt a tremendous rush take over his body. His heart beat faster, his breath became ragged and his thoughts started to wander. He daydreamed of fishing from his decked out Jon Boat on the Chattahoochee River...The trees, the sun, the white-foamed moving water running fresh air and new life to everything around it...Trout, bass, catfish – all splashing around his boat at once. Out of nowhere, the fish started jumping into his lap one by one without even casting a line. *Bitchin' place*, he thought to himself. *Bass Master Scarborough has arrived.*

In the real world, Wesley was passed out cold on the floor in front of his stereo. His eyes sealed shut. His legendary grin, frozen on his face. The loud rock music pummeled his crack-laced-with-PCP flooded body into a black, motionless, faded existence.

CHAPTER 5

And So It Begins...

SATURDAY, JANUARY 26, 1991
3:03 A.M.

P<small>OP!!!</small>

What was that? Wesley's eyes jolted open.

Still on the floor, he tried to move his body, but his soul was detached. Every body part paralyzed except for his cerulean blue eyes that struggled to stay open. He summoned all of his strength and managed to roll over to see the origin of that horrible sound. He looked down to the opposite end of his bedroom...

Oh my God. This can't be happening.

Wesley blinked his eyes hard and looked again. There on his bed, was David by the headboard, gun in hand, with his knees pinning Ava's stretched out arms; Ava, naked and struggling, lying spread-eagled beneath him, with her dark bushy pubic hair embarrassingly visible to everyone in the room; Sebastian, kneeling at the other end of the bed, using his body weight to pin down Ava's kicking legs, as he unbuckled the belt from his pants.

In that instant, everything turned to slow motion. *Stop it!!! Please!!! Not Her!!!* Wesley tried calling out several times, but nothing came out of his mouth...

Not one fucking sound.

Paralyzed on the floor, he helplessly watched Sebastian climb onto Ava, pull her knees into the air and force himself *into* her like a rabid dog fucking a dying puppy. Wesley simply watched...helplessly...as his eyelids became heavier and heavier...

Until he passed into darkness once again.

CHAPTER 6

DREAMS I'LL NEVER SEE

SATURDAY, JANUARY 26, 1991
4:08 A.M.

"Come on, Wes," Emma's girlish high voice echoed through the room. "Wake up, baby, you're missing it!"

Wesley opened his eyes and saw his beautiful blonde girlfriend directly beneath him. "What's wrong, baby?"

They were in the middle of having sex.

"What's your problem?" she asked. "Keep going."

Wesley vacillated for a moment. His body ached all over, like he'd been beaten with a concrete bat. He gathered all his energy to continue making love to Emma, missionary style.

"That's it, boy. Keep going," she said.

"I had a terrible dream," he whispered back.

"Who cares, Wes, just keep going." Emma's caramel brown eyes stared back at him as her long, blonde hair overwhelmed his black satin pillowcase.

Wesley thought Emma was the perfect long-distance girlfriend. She was rich, pretty and stupid as homemade

West Virginian sin. So stupid in fact that while travel-
ing with her family in France, she sent Wesley a postcard
where she placed her address in the middle of the card and
his information in the upper left hand *return address* corner.
It was upon receiving that postcard four months later that
Wesley knew he could never marry her. He knew he would
get bored of her too easily, just like he was bored of her
now. But Wesley would never admit this fact to anyone,
especially his mother. For it was her who had insisted he
marry young and start a family, so that one day soon, like
his famous father, he could sit on the bench and rule.

Wesley finally gave in to Emma and started letting go.
What the hell, he said to himself, grinding his angled hips
into her perfectly tanned stomach.

"That's it, Wes…keep it up, just like that…" her brown
eyes still looking directly into his. "Just ride the bitch,
Wes…Ride that bitch like she deserves it."

"What?"

"Fuck the bitch harder, Wes!" she screamed.

Wesley was now totally perplexed. Usually, Emma
was silent and moved like wet cardboard. She continued
squirming with pleasure underneath him, but this time,
Sebastian's deep voice came out of her.

"I wanna see you make her bleed, Wes. Make her bleed like a stuck pig."

Wesley stopped. He panicked. He leapt out of bed and looked around the room. On his right he saw Sebastian and David, sharing the red overstuffed chair, cheering him on.

"Why'd you stop Wes? Get back in there!" howled Sebastian.

Terrified, Wesley looked back into the bed. Emma was never there; it was Ava all along. Her mouth taped shut with silver duct tape. Her dark hair ripped out and scattered around the black pillowcase beneath her. Her scalp, cheek and vagina smeared with blood. Yet hauntingly, it was her large, empty eyes that destroyed Wesley from the inside out. Her eyes flickering between staying in this painful life or moving on to peaceful death…pleading, praying, screaming, calling, crying, begging, begging, begging…*Why, Wesley? Why?*

Wesley's face melted into pure horror.

His head hit the floor *hard*.

CHAPTER 7

THE AFTERMATH

SATURDAY, JANUARY 26, 1991
2:23 P.M.

A car honked loudly outside. Five seconds later, it honked again.

Wesley awoke on the floor, this time in front of his bright bedroom window. As he opened his eyes, he caught sight of the stereo clock ten feet away. *Holy shit.* He remembered he had promised his mother dinner this evening and realized he only had a few hours to get his shit together. He touched his long, greasy-gold hair, feeling that it was tangled in knots, especially at the back of his head. He gazed down at his body, relieved that he was at least wearing a pair of boxer shorts: the solid, dark red ones that his girlfriend gave him this past Christmas. Truth is, Wesley felt as if he had been ran over a hundred times by a Tiananmen Square tank, yet somehow he was still alive and completely lucid.

Now that he was fully awake, he caught wind of the horrific stink emanating from his body. *What the hell happened last night?*

Wesley struggled to remember the details: *dinner at Martoni, war party at Zeta House, hung out with history girl, partied hard with the guys. What else?* In that moment, all he could feel was mega-hangover pain pulsating throughout his body. In response, he launched his Saturday morning mantra:

I swear to you, Heavenly Father, if you get me through this day without repercussion, I will change my evil ways and never, ever touch drugs or alcohol again.

Sure, Wesley. We'll see about that.

The car outside honked long and loud this third time around.

Curious as to where the noise was coming from, Wesley managed to pull himself up the windowsill and peeked through the oak plantation blinds. Outside, he watched Mrs. Lipton power-hobble her way down to a running Mercedes-Benz in her circular driveway. "Please hurry, Mrs. Lipton," he said softly. "Stop the honking. Please."

As Wesley moved his hand away from the window, he noticed something on the blinds. It was blood. He raised his hand up to his sunlit face, examining it closely: *dried blood?* He looked down his entire chest and body, zeroing in on his boxer shorts. Suddenly, he realized he wasn't wearing his dark red boxer shorts after all. He was wearing his *white* ones, which had somehow stained red in the front overnight. *Holy shit.*

Wesley turned to look down to the other end of the sun-filled room. There was no sound. No movement. Yet the image he saw on *his bed* caused his breath to nearly stop. His heart started beating out of his chest. His lower extremities cringed with *fear*, a fear that quickly climbed up Wesley's spine, into the base of his neck and exploded onto his face.

Oh my God!!!!

Wesley's hands trembled as he rushed to peel off the waistband of his stuck-to-his-skin red boxer shorts, throwing them down his legs and quickly stepping out of them. While nude, Wesley carefully inspected his larger than average penis. Holding it up high, twisting it, confirming there was no injury he could see despite being splattered with what looked like the remnants of a broken jar of rotten marinara sauce. He grabbed a pair of clean, gray boxer shorts off the floor. He continued shaking while changing, quickly replacing the dirty boxer shorts with the clean sin-less ones.

Once finished, Wesley walked in tight circles, holding his bloody boxer shorts in his hand. *Where to hide them?* The pressure emanating from brain to temple was excru-ciating. For the first time, Wesley felt real stress, the kind of stress soldiers feel when under live, aggressive attack versus the *I'm stressed out because of traffic* yuppie bullshit. This was real adrenaline, the fight or flight super-power that kept our ancestors alive when saber-toothed tigers wanted man-snack for breakfast. And Wesley needed it now to stay alive in this very moment.

He finally decided to hide the bloody boxer shorts be-hind the right stereo speaker five steps in front of him. He then spotted a half-empty bottle of water on the floor. He rapidly opened it and dumped it on his hands, rubbing them together with all of his might. It was too late for that. The blood was so dried upon his skin it looked like it had been there for weeks. Now that it was wet again, it had a slightly coppery smell, like a public restroom trashcan filled with dirty tampons. For a moment, Wesley gazed at his blood-covered hands, still reeling from the initial shock of finding himself in such a pointless, grave situation. As soon as Wesley snapped out of it, he sprinted over to the other side of the room with the intention of waking the others.

Sebastian lay asleep in Wesley's overstuffed red chair, shirtless. His rolling folds of pale white fat rising and falling with each slumbering breath. Fortunately, he was wearing his half-zippered, perfectly pressed khaki dress pants, pristine and untainted with blood.

"Sebastian, wake up. Sebastian!"

Sebastian cracked a slit in his eye and realized who it was. "What's up?" he said with a broken, phlegmy voice.

"We've got a real fucking problem. Get up."

The look on Wesley's face propped open Sebastian's pale blue fish eyes like a springboard. "What's going on?"

Wesley turned his head and looked at the bed. Sebastian's eyes followed.

"What the…Holy shit."

"Yeah. Holy Mother of God fucking shit!"

Sebastian straightened up, leaned back to zipper his pants then jetted straight out of his chair. He had gotten up so fast that he had become dizzy. "Where's David?"

"I don't know."

They both looked around the room intently.

Wesley noticed a large hump sleeping underneath the black and gold jacquard covers. "David!!!"

He didn't move. Wesley rushed over to the side of the bed, pulled the comforter down and rattled him violently. "David, wake up!"

"Get the fuck up, David!"

David moved a quarter inch. His breath was warm and smelled like garbage. "C'mon y'all. Let me sleep," he replied, without even opening his eyes.

"Get your crackhead ass out of that bed and put some clothes on. Right. Fucking. Now!" commanded Sebastian from several feet away.

David sluggishly opened his eyes and noticed Wesley's panic-stricken face looking just beyond his shoulder. "What's next to me?" he asked, fearful of the answer.

"It's that girl." Wesley couldn't even speak her given name.

David reluctantly moved to see what was lying next to him, rolling over ever so slowly. Once he made eye contact with what shared his bed, he *jumped* to his feet, his dick and nut sack warped with blood, fully on display. David jittered so hard he looked like a kernel in oil, ready to jump through his skin. "Whaaah, whah, what are we gonna do?"

"Fuck, David. We don't know," replied Wesley. "Put some clothes on."

Instead, all three men just stood there, staring at what was in the bed. Sebastian was repulsed, David was petrified and Wesley was worried beyond words.

Wesley started to pace the room. His feet landed so hard they thudded with every step against the dark cherry wood floor. "Think y'all. Think!"

"Think what, Wes?" Sebastian's breathing was now deep and labored.

"We've got to fucking *think*!"

"What are we gonna do?" whimpered David.

"I don't fucking know yet! Can't you see I'm still thinking?"

Sebastian hesitated. "Is she dead?"

"I don't know." Wesley gestured to David to go check.

"Hell no, I ain't going near that!"

"Fucking *do* it, David!"

"Do it!"

David's skinny, naked chest shivered even faster as he walked back over to the bed. When he arrived, he looked down and hesitated.

"Take it off! We need to see her fucking face!" commanded Sebastian.

"Do it!"

Scrunching his eyes to avoid looking down, David struggled to pull something up from the bed. After a few hard tugs, he pulled up a white bloody pillowcase.

"Oh my God."

"We're fucked."

David began to cry.

"Check to see if she's breathing."

"She's fucking *dead*, Wes!"

"Fucking check!"

David hesitated. He drew a deep breath, shivered it out and then drew a deeper breath, holding it before quickly bending down to the bed to listen. Seconds later, he popped back up. "I think she's still breathing."

"Shit."

"Shit?"

"I'm not going to jail, Wes!"

"Well you should've thought about that before you fucking did this!"

"As I recall, you didn't have a problem fucking her either."

Wesley reacted at first with confusion, then tremendous guilt. Suddenly small details of what happened the previous night began to emerge.

He continued to pace the room...

"Put some fucking clothes on, David. You're embarrassing."

"I can't. I'm too scared."

Wesley interrupted his pacing, marched over to his open closet, ripped a pair of acid wash jeans from the hanger and threw them at David who was too weak to catch them.

"Give me that pillow, David, will you?" asked Sebastian.

"What are you doing?"

"Throw me the fucking pillow!"

David grabbed a large red fringe pillow from the bed and lobbed it to Sebastian.

"What the hell are you doing?"

"I'm not going to jail, Wes!"

Sebastian moved toward the bed with pillow in hand, ready to use it as a murder weapon.

"NOOOOOOO!!!"

Wesley tackled Sebastian, wrestling him to the floor, best friends since childhood punching each other along the way. "You fucking did this!" exclaimed Sebastian in between punches.

"Stop it, y'all! Stop it!" whimpered David. He ran over, naked and jiggling, managing to pull the much bigger Sebastian away from Wesley.

"Get off of me, you prick."

After a few long breaths on the ground, Wesley raised himself from the floor. He wiped the blood from a cut on his chin. At the same time, Sebastian went to the bed and searched for the small black gun he'd left there overnight. He picked it up and aimed it directly at Wesley.

"You should've never brought the damn bitch here, Wes."

David was terrified.

"C'mon, Sebastian, we just got way too high, that's all."

"It's your fault we're in this shit, Wes. *Your fault!*"

"Now hold on, Sebastian. We're all in this shit together," he reasoned.

"Fuck you!" His strawberry eyebrows crossed in rage. "How many times have I tried to stop you from chasing charity pussy, Wes? Tell me! How many fucking times?"

David started crying. "Please, y'all. I can't take this."

Sebastian pointed the gun at David. "Stop crying!"

David quieted down. Sebastian returned his aim at Wesley.

"Look, Sebastian…"

"I knew something like this was bound to happen because of you. I just fucking *knew* it."

"Sebastian…See that gun right there, in your hands? You know it's mine, right? Registered to me."

"So what?"

"That's *my* gun, this is *my* house and that's *my* date dying on the fucking bed. Who do you think they're gonna come after when they find her body? Huh? Not you, man. Not David. They're gonna come after *me*. I'm the only one who's in deep shit here!"

Sebastian slowly started to get his point.

"I swear to you on the lives of my fucking unborn children, I will get us all out of this. Just put the gun down and let me think. Please."

After a beat, Sebastian put the gun down.

David started to cry.

"Shut up, you're not helping!"

A slight groan came from the bed. They all turned and looked.

"We need to get her to a hospital," said Wesley.

"What, call 911 and say we all gang-banged some chick last night and now she ain't doing so hot? Wes, think about what you're saying! We can't take her to a fucking hospital."

Wesley continued to pace in his gray boxer shorts. David grabbed the acid wash jeans from the floor, sniffling quietly as he put them on.

Suddenly, Wesley came up with an idea. "Someone else can take her. Let's drop her off somewhere."

"Where?"

"We'll put her in the car and leave her downtown. Somewhere busy."

"Wes, people saw us at the Zeta House together. They saw us leave together. Our fucking neighbor even saw us walk in here with her last night."

"But who's to say she *stayed* here all night?"

Sebastian reacted as if he had a point. "But what about...our stuff?"

"What stuff?"

"Our sweat! Our cum! Our saliva!"

"We'll clean her up. Alcohol, peroxide, we'll fix her up best we can. They won't be able to find a damn thing on her body."

"And what about *the inside?*" Sebastian looked at the others with deep concern.

After a loud sniffle, David finally spoke up. "My Momma left her turkey baster here at Thanksgiving."

Wesley and Sebastian immediately exchanged a look: *what a damn good idea.*

In the kitchen, Sebastian rummaged through several cabinets. Nothing. He then combed through an overcrowded utensil drawer. He dug his hand deep into the back of the drawer, finally pulling out a foot-long, metal turkey baster with an orange rubber bulb.

In the hallway, David rifled through a large storage closet. He pulled out towels, cotton, washcloths, alcohol, witch hazel, peroxide – as much as he could hold in his arms.

In the laundry room, Sebastian swung open a cabinet over the washing machine. He whipped out a large, wide mouth bottle of chlorine bleach and slammed it on top of the dryer. He flipped the cap open, stuck the turkey baster inside and squeezed the orange bulb.

In the bedroom, Wesley hurriedly laid down extra white sheets on the bed, keeping the body warm. "It's going to be okay," he whispered. "Just hang on, sweet girl. Please."

David burst through the bedroom door, throwing all of the items he was carrying onto the bed, right next to Wesley. "That's everything."

"Where's Sebastian?"

Sebastian's large silhouette stood in the doorway with the daunting foot-long metal turkey baster in hand. "I'm ready." Just as he moved toward the bed, Wesley intervened.

"Wait. What if it kills her?"

"We're running out of fucking time, Wes!"

DING DONG DING.

Holy shit. The doorbell rang.

They froze in place and looked at one another. After a few seconds of silence, it rang again. "It's my mother." Wesley moved as if he were going to answer the door.

"Don't fucking answer it," said Sebastian in a loud whisper.

"She's got keys to the front door," replied Wesley in a louder whisper.

David quietly crumbled. "What if it's the police?"

"Stop that shit now, David."

"Just stay calm. I'll fucking handle this."

Wesley grabbed a black ZZ Top concert shirt from his middle dresser drawer and headed toward the living room.

DING DONG DING.

Wesley opened the front door. It was Miss Eloise, a large sixty-year-old black woman with a personality as big as her waistline. She stood on the porch wearing a traditional French maid uniform, holding a bucket of cleaning products in her hand.

"Good Afternoon, Wesley."

"Miss Eloise? I'm sorry, I, I wasn't expecting you."

"I hate to barge in, but your mother wanted me to swing by and clean up your house this afternoon. She said something about Maria getting deported last week?"

"Oh, yes, Maria. Oh, uh, no, no problem. I mean, we're cool. We don't need your help today. You should take the afternoon off. Aren't you cold without a coat?"

"Not the way I work up a sweat, child, you know that."

Wesley moved to hide the dried blood on his hands.

"You feelin' all right, son?"

"Yes, ma'am. I'm fine. Just had a long night."

Miss Eloise turned around and looked at the unfamiliar yellow car parked right in front of the house. "Yes, I can see that."

Shit. I forgot about Ava's car!

"Yes, ma'am. Long night."

Sebastian was crouched at the foot of the waterbed with the turkey baster raised in his right hand. His chest was lifted and his eyes were focused, ready to perform the sadistic gynecological cleaning procedure. David was immediately beside him, trembling over his shoulder. "Okay. Here we go…"

"But how did you hurt your hand, Wesley? Let me take a look at it."

"Oh, no, I'm fine. I just got in a fight last night. At a bar. I'm fine."

"*You* in a fight? Over what?" Eloise cracked a nostalgic smile. "The girl who drives *that* ugly car?"

Wesley returned an awkward smile.

"You remind me so much of your daddy before he met your mother. Whew, Lord! If you only knew the bachelor stories I got locked up in my secret box. But those come with me to the grave, ya hear?"

Wesley once again faked a pleasant smile.

Sebastian slowly rose from the foot of the bed, his eyes wide open and filled with panic.

"What...the?"

The empty turkey baster rolled from his hand, down to the floor.

David started to cry.

"In this day and age, playing with the wrong lady friend can get you killed. I know you know what I'm talkin' about."

"Yes, Miss Eloise."

"I'm serious, Wesley. This AIDS thing ain't no joke. They say regular people can get it now too."

"Yes, ma'am. I know that."

"Well, okay then. I understand you don't want to be disturbed right now, so I'll come back tomorrow after church. Just make sure you've asked your lady friend to leave by then."

"Yes, ma'am. I will. Thank you."

Wesley awkwardly waved good-bye to Miss Eloise as she turned to walk back down the porch. As fast as he could, he closed the door and locked it. When he turned around, he saw a shirtless David standing in the living room: speechless, crying and hyperventilating.

Wesley sprinted into the bedroom.

As he entered, his face contorted into pure horror.

"What the fuck is *happening* to her???"

Ava's naked, grotesque body was convulsing violently on the bed. Her skin, blackened and bloody, oozing clear liquid against the white sheets like a piece of barbeque chicken leaking onto a thin paper plate. Her legs were spread wide and distorted, her dark brown bush of pubic hair clumped with dried red matter. Her waist, mustard yellow and blue from bruising, her small pink breast nipples on the floor, cut off, leaving gaping holes that had coagulated into black scabs overnight. Her pale arms, limp and lifeless, while her torso rose up and down, seizuring, lifting inches above the bed. Her head, heavy and weighed down, attached to the black satin pillow, her white scalp showing through the ripped out pieces of her dark reddish-brown hair. The whole scene looked like an invisible bowling ball crushing a struggling spider. But her face... Her face was most affected. Mangled and disfigured, both eyes swollen tight like wontons filled with blood, her classical nose now leaning over to the side, broken and discharging, her motionless lips covered by three peeling strips of silver duct tape. Yes, a horrible face attached to a mutilated body – shaking, jumping, convulsing violently on the bed.

"Oh my God, she's dying!"

"Get her in the fucking car now!!!"

David stood alone on the curb as Wesley's BMW screeched off in pure daylight. His skinny, shirtless chest shivered in the light, cold wind.

Wesley drove fast on the highway with Sebastian slumped down beside him in the passenger seat. His face was square with determination, his eyes possessed by lack of sleep.

"Okay. Let's do it," said Sebastian, defeated.

Wesley pulled his BMW into the hospital emergency room drop off area. He leaned on the car horn as it echoed through the concrete pavilion.

In the lobby, Wesley spoke into a payphone while Sebastian stood by his side listening intently. "No, no, I'm not hurt! Please listen! You don't understand what's going on. I just need you to come down here right now." Wesley's voice cracked...

"Momma, I'm in *big* trouble."

CHAPTER 8

The Awakening

WEDNESDAY, FEBRUARY 6, 1991
9:23 A.M.

"I want you to throw him in jail. I want that boy to pay!"

Ava slowly opened her eyes. Her very first fuzzy image was that of a television located high above in the corner of a hospital room. On the screen, a blonde woman dressed in a green, seventies era Diane Von Furstenberg wrap dress was flailing around, screaming at a cop dressed in traditional blues. "I need you to arrest him, officer. Arrest him now!"

With eyes still out of focus, Ava slowly moved her gaze across the hospital room. She was able to make out three separate vases of colorful, but dead flowers on the table beside her. Next to that, she noticed a batch of deflated Mylar balloons puking cheerful sayings like "Get Well Soon" and "Hang In There." She then looked at the loud tan metal machine she was attached to, making out the numbers 105/75 in neon green letters on the screen, and the clear IV line pumping something important into her veins. But what truly caught her attention was a large yellow object sitting on a chair in the corner. She sharpened her focus and realized it was a yellow, five-foot-tall teddy bear, with perky ears and a huge smile on its face. Its custom made plastic chest read "We Love You, Ava!" in sweet bubble face rainbow letters. There was only one person in the world who would have brought that teddy bear as a gift. And that man was sitting two feet away from her, watching the blonde lady in the sky yelling.

Forty-eight-year-old Nick DeSantis was the kind of New York City tough guy you would never want to owe money to. His thirty years in the gaming industry turned him from an aggressive, unpredictable, mob-affiliated youth, into a reliable, upstanding, tax-paying good guy. Let's face it. Working under constant camera surveillance can turn anyone into a rule-abiding citizen, but it was the unexpected death of his wife, Bevin McCauley DeSantis, that truly changed Nick at his core.

Nick and Bevin had been childhood sweethearts. The *perfect* odd couple: a lovely, foul-mouthed Irish girl crazy in love with the volatile, hot-headed Greek guy. They even shared a birthday – September 25th – and married the day they both turned eighteen. Nick and Bevin had always wanted a big family even though it had been a struggle. In fact, they had been together for more than a decade before their precious baby Ava even came along.

For years, Nick was angry with God for taking his soulmate and leaving him to raise his daughter alone. But Bevin's spirit would visit Nick in his dreams, inspiring him to change his violent ways and become a loving and stable father to Ava. For he too came from a large family and was beyond grateful to have at least one child, spoiling her best he could with Boardwalk toys and stuffed animals, until her small bedroom was overflowing with a sea of fur babies and plastic dolls.

Bevin always knew Nick was a good man at heart. "A good man dealt a bad hand," she would say to him in his dreams. At her funeral, Nick quietly swore to her spirit that he would never remarry. He promised her that he would always take care of Ava, making sure this cruel world never touched her the way it did his wife. Unfortunately, Nick was not able to keep that promise. Not today. Not ever.

Ava was pleased to see her father sitting beside her in a chair, watching a *Colombo* re-run on the television. Grungy and unshaven, it was obvious he had been wearing the same maroon Members Only jacket and dark Jordache jeans for days.

Nick casually glanced down at Ava to check on her. Suddenly, his weary expression turned into pure joy. "Nurse," he spoke into the call button. "Nurse! Nurse!!!"

"Yes?"

"My daughter. Her eyes are open!"

"I'll get the doctor right away."

"Tell her to haul ass!"

Nick turned and smiled back at Ava. "Hey, Pumpkin, it's me. Can you hear me in there?"

Ava looked like a Halloween party mummy, wrapped from head to thigh in snow-white gauze bandages. The only body parts peeking through the mummy mask were her large eyes (marbled green and red with blood), and her full, pale lips cracked and chapped from the lack of orally administered liquids for the past eleven days.

"You have no idea how hard I've been praying to your mother, kiddo. Thank God she heard me."

Ava stared at her father with confusion. She knew why she was there. She just couldn't figure out why there was a dull, aching pain radiating from her stomach.

Doctor Jennifer Morris, a caring, thirty-six-year-old black woman that had obviously graduated from the Oprah Winfrey School of Medicine, entered the room.

"Ava! I'm so glad you finally decided to join us. I was afraid you were going to sleep through the entire party and miss all the fun we're having."

Ava tried pointlessly to respond.

"My name is Doctor Morris, but please call me Jennifer. The whole *doctor* thing makes me feel old." She showcased a wide, bright smile against her flawless dark skin. "I'll be your physician here during your stay."

Ava's eyes responded politely.

Doctor Morris grabbed a medical chart from the holder at the foot of the bed. Simultaneously, the nurse entered the room and smiled at Ava. "Well, hello there, Miss DeSantis. Good Morning."

Doctor Morris quickly turned around and spoke in a stern whisper. "Please call Detective Zhao and let him know she's awake." The nurse nodded and exited right away.

"Now, Ava, I know that talking is a little tough for you right now, but not to worry, you'll be gabbing away again very soon. In the meantime, do you think you can write down a few things for me?"

Ava slowly nodded her mummy head: *yes*

"Wonderful!" Doctor Morris walked over to the night-stand. She picked up a metal clipboard and a black marker, placing it on Ava's lap. "Now, I want you to take your time writing because it may be a little difficult at first. This is not a test. Spelling doesn't count. This is just your way to communicate for a little while, okay?"

Ava nodded.

"Great. Now, I know you probably feel sore all over, which is perfectly normal, but is there any specific area of your body that's causing you *serious* pain?"

Ava tried to grip the black marker, struggling to hold it between her fingers. Doctor Morris placed her hand over Ava's to assist her. "That's it. Take your time."

Unable to stomach the scene, Nick briefly turned away and looked at the brick wall so Ava wouldn't see the tears welling in his eyes.

With Doctor Morris's help, Ava finally gripped the black marker. The first word she wrote down was: HEAD

"Ahh, yes. That's because you suffered a nasty concussion right here," Doctor Morris touched the left side of her head. "That is your temporal lobe which controls speech and memory. Explains why you're having a little trouble talking now, doesn't it?"

Ava nodded: *yes*.

"But I promise you, in a few days, your head will start to feel better, okay? Now, do you feel pain anywhere else?"

Ava wrote down: CHEST

Doctor Morris looked at Nick for a brief moment.

"Yes, we took care of that one as soon as you arrived. We had to clean out the infection in both breasts, but we made it all better. Feels really itchy, doesn't it?"

Ava nodded: *yes*.

"That's from the stiches. Luckily, no major arteries were severed so we were able to sew you back up just fine. I'll take out the stiches in about three more days, but for now, we'll use an ointment to stop the itching. Okay?"

Ava conveyed a sense of relief through her eyes.

"Is there anything else? Anything causing you serious pain, Ava?"

Ava looked nervously at Doctor Morris, then at her father. Doctor Morris shot Nick a look that said, *please excuse us.*

"Pumpkin, I'm going to run downstairs and get some coffee. I'll be back soon." Nick rose from his plastic chair and left the hospital room.

Doctor Morris's upbeat tone suddenly became more serious. "Ava, the reason you hurt down there is that you suffered a serious chemical injury to your cervix and part of your uterus. The damage was extensive and you are definitely lucky to be alive. But the good news is that we have already performed the surgery to repair the tissue that—"

Ava quickly scribbled down: BABIES?

Doctor Morris hesitated. Her expression said it all. "Ava, I'm sorry. I did everything I could."

Her eyes screamed disappointment beyond description.

"Ava, I know this is tough news but there are many alternatives to explore when the day comes that you want to become a mother…"

She turned her head and looked away.

"Ava, you do not have to give birth to a child to be that child's mother."

Tears now streamed down her face, wetting the bandages that hid them.

"Just think about how much you loved your mother, Ava. Would you have loved her any less if she didn't give birth to you?"

She suddenly burst out sobbing behind the bandage mask.

"Ava...I..."

Ava continued to cry, wailing out loud.

Moved by the heart-wrenching sound of muffled tears, Doctor Morris became emotional as well. She grabbed a tissue from the nightstand and dabbed Ava's eyes. She then grabbed another tissue and dabbed away her own tears.

"I'll get the nurse to change these out for you just as soon as you're done, so go ahead and let it all out now."

Ava continued to cry about losing her ability to hold *her own baby* in her arms. The news hit her so hard that it ripped a hole inside her core. For years, having a baby was all she could think about, especially after her own mother passed away. With only three goals in life (graduate from college, become a history teacher and find a wonderful husband to give her at least four bouncing babies) she felt as if the world took away the most important job a woman can list on her resume: *mother*.

Ava sobbed so loudly that hospital workers in the hallway peeked through the small interior window to see what was creating that pitiful, sad, sad sound.

Doctor Morris gathered herself and continued her speech: "Ava, you have *no idea* how lucky you are to even be alive. You've already made it through the worst part, so don't give up on me now, girl." She faked a smile through her own tears.

Ava was instantly comforted by her gentleness.

"Now, tell me, is there anything else causing you pain? Anything we missed? I want you to heal your best and get out of here better than ever."

Ava shook her head: *no*.

"Good. That's great. Now, there's one last thing I need to ask you...I have a friend that wants to speak with you. Do you think you're up to meeting him today?"

Ava hesitated, then wrote down: WHO?

"His name is Rudy Zhao. He's a detective with the sexual assault unit."

Ava's hand did not move.

Doctor Morris sat on the edge of the bed. "Ava, two young men found you naked, lying in the road next to your car. They said they didn't know you well, but they recognized you from school. Do you remember any of this?"

Ava's eyes filled with fear. She remembered everything.

Doctor Morris drew a deep breath then continued. "When I asked them if they knew the phone number to Anniston so I could locate your parents, one of the boys told me that your mother was deceased and that your father lived in Atlantic City."

Ava did not respond.

"Ava, if that young man didn't know you, how could he have known where your father lived? And why was he so upset when he brought you in? The boy literally dropped to his knees in the waiting room and begged me to save your life."

Ava looked away, refusing to answer.

"What I haven't told you yet is that I specialize in treating patients like you. I know something *horrible* happened that night, but I can't help you until you tell Detective Zhao all of the details."

Ava's eyes begged for mercy. It was too much, too soon.

"All right, we don't have to talk about it now." Doctor Morris touched the clipboard and marker. "I'll let you keep this on your lap so if you feel like writing something down, please do so, okay?"

Ava nodded: *yes.*

"Now is there absolutely anything else you need before I go for a little while?"

Ava wrote down: H2O

Doctor Morris smiled. "You got it. Just press this call button anytime you need something, okay?" She raised from the bed. "And get some rest. I'll check on you again shortly." Doctor Morris affectionately looked at Ava as she exited the hospital room.

The nurse stood outside Ava's room, watching her through the little window. "How did she take the news?"

"Not very well. Neither did I," replied Doctor Morris.

"What a shame. She's so young."

"Oh, and before I forget, she asked for some water."

The nurse nodded, then turned to walk.

"Also, please call Detective Zhao and tell him to forget about coming down today." She looked at Ava through the window. "This one's not going to talk for a *long* time."

CHAPTER 9

THE DEVIL WENT DOWN TO GEORGIA

WEDNESDAY, FEBRUARY 6, 1991
11:03 A.M.

Ava picked up the clipboard from her lap. She flipped it around and looked at her distorted mummy reflection in the metal mirror. Just then, Nick re-entered the room.

"Hey, Pumpkin. Are you all through with the doctor?"

Ava put the clipboard down on her lap and nodded: *yes*.

"Good, I want you to meet someone."

Ava cringed. She was in no condition to communicate with anyone else, let alone a sexual assault detective. But to her surprise, a petite, well-dressed, big-haired blonde woman wearing a bright red business suit entered the room. She was carrying an over-the-top flower arrangement that was so large it covered most of her face.

"Pumpkin, I want you to meet—"

The nurse abruptly entered the room with Ava's bottle of water. Nick and his mystery guest stood awkwardly silent until the nursed finished placing the water on the nightstand, then exited. The blonde woman placed the flowers beside the water bottle and began to speak.

"Hello, Ava. My name is Miriam. I'm Wesley's mother."

Ava nearly jumped out of her skin.

Miriam Scarborough was a forty-five-year-old strikingly beautiful, church going steel magnolia who couldn't get into Heaven even if she gave Saint Michael a blowjob. In addition to being the richest and most active member of her century-old Baptist church, Miriam was also a *Davenport*, a well-known Confederate family that helped found Atlanta back in 1847. But what was most interesting about Miriam was that despite her inherited wealth, she had attended law school at a time where nice Southern ladies stayed out of such sticky matters, let alone grow up to become the highest paid criminal defense attorney in all of Fulton County.

"It's okay, Pumpkin, Mrs. Scarborough just wants to talk to you." Nick's voice was oddly authoritative given the circumstances.

Ava was unsure of how to respond.

Miriam drew a deep breath, and then hesitated. "I'm sorry, Nick. I didn't expect this visit to be so difficult."

After a few moments of stale silence, Nick jumped in and got straight to the point. "Pumpkin, you didn't write down anything to the doctor about how you got here, did you?"

Ava gently shook her head: *no.*

Nick and Miriam exchanged a look of relief.

"Ava, I know that we do not personally know one another, but I want you to know from the bottom of my heart that I do not judge you in *any* way. Wesley tells me that you are a very smart girl, and what you do behind closed doors in no way affects my opinion of you."

Ava was confused by her words.

Miriam drew another fake deep breath and continued her speech: "I know you are wondering and yes, Wesley told me *everything.* As a mother, it was probably the most painful thing my only son has ever told me, but the good Lord knows how things like this can happen when alcohol is involved. I'm sure you can remember that you drank a little too much that night. Am I right, sugar?"

Ava felt a pang of guilt in her stomach.

"Now this doesn't mean you are a bad person whatsoever. You are just an innocent victim like the millions of other young girls out there who throw their virginity to any sweet man who buys them a drink. Everyone in this room knows alcohol is just the Devil's way of making good people like you do his dirty work. And I am sure beyond the shadow of a doubt that you would have never convinced the other boys to play that…that…*God forsaken sex game* if you hadn't been drinking so much alcohol."

Miriam became emotional. Nick consoled her.

Ava stared at the scene before her in disbelief.

Miriam slowly pulled herself together. "Ava, I beg of you, as one Christian to another, please consider keeping this mishap just between us."

Ava was frozen.

"I'm afraid, since our name is so well known in this town, that if you tell anyone about what happened, the media will surely get a hold of it. All the tabloids, the local TV stations, the national papers, everyone will write a story about this." Miriam moved closer to Ava and leaned in only inches away from her mummified face. "Ava, you strike me as a private person. Do you really want everyone to know you had sex with three men at the same time?"

Ava was taken aback.

"Do you really want to read about yourself in the papers, Ava? Everyone at Anniston University will know. Your childhood friends in New Jersey will know. Everyone will know your name, Ava. The media will slaughter your reputation like they did with Jessica Hahn, Donna Rice... Their lives are destroyed forever."

Nick shot Miriam a dirty look that said: *take it easy.*

"Do you really want your father to have to read ugly lies about you, Ava? About your family? I'm sure your sweet mother in Heaven is looking down on us right this very second, crying her eyes out into Jesus's arms."

"That's enough." Nick had reached his limit. "Do not speak about my wife. Ever."

"I'm sorry, Nick. I, I didn't mean to offend. I just know as a mother I would hate to see your daughter ruin her life for just one little mistake."

"Just get to the point, Mrs. Scarborough. Please."

Miriam squared her shoulders and went in for the kill. "Ava, what's done is done. None of us can change the past, but we all have the power to change the future. Do you understand what I am saying?"

Ava gently shook her head: *no.*

"Ava, if you agree to keep this between us, I promise you that I will take care of you for the rest of your life. As soon as you leave here, you can move back to New Jersey, get your own apartment, spend time with your friends—"

Nick interrupted. "Baby, Mrs. Scarborough was nice enough to pay for all of this. You and me, we don't have health insurance."

Ava was surprised at her father's revelation.

"Yes, Ava, I have arranged with your father to cover all of your medical expenses. Not just the tens of thousands you are incurring every single day you stay here, but also your future medical expenses. I know you don't want to be a financial burden on your father, Ava. Plus it will take years to repair your f..." Miriam caught herself before saying it. "What I mean to say is that I will pay for the best plastic surgeon in all of New Jersey. And I promise you he or she will restore that lovely face of yours and make you prettier than ever."

Ava was terrified. It never even occurred to her what her face must look like under the mummy mask.

"Ava, God has blessed me with an amazing family. When my father passed last year, he left me more money than any one person could ever spend in a lifetime. Which is why I am willing to share my blessings with you. Specifically, I will wire your father five hundred thousand dollars the minute you return to your home in New Jersey. And, in fifteen years, I will wire you another five hundred thousand dollars."

Ava was floored.

"That's one million dollars in total, Ava. More than you could ever hope to earn as a teacher in a lifetime."

Ava's eyes pleaded to Nick for help.

"And all I ask from you in return is that you keep this misunderstanding between us. Nothing more. Just never say another word to another soul and we will all be fine."

Ava was shocked.

"Pumpkin, all you need to do is promise to keep this between the three of us. It's as simple as that."

Ava could not believe what her father was saying. The man who stood by his principles no matter what the cost… the man who always said rich people were evil and should never be trusted, was now the man standing side by side with a woman willing to part with a million dollars to keep her privileged son out of prison.

For a good twenty seconds, a heavy, sick feeling of silence filled the room.

"I should go. I'll leave you two alone to think this over." Miriam turned and looked directly at Nick. "All I ask is that if your daughter decides to speak to the police, that you will at least call me in advance so that I may prepare my family."

"Of course." said Nick. "That's the least we can do."

Miriam turned back and looked directly at Ava. "I know you will make the right decision, Ava. You are a very smart girl." Miriam turned to leave once more. "And thank you both for listening to me. I pray we can all work this out."

Soon after Miriam left, Nick pulled his chair a foot away from Ava and rubbed his scruffy dark chin. "Pumpkin, do you remember about a month after your mother died, you were getting ready to start school again, and you got your hair cut so short that you looked like a boy?"

Her eyes welled with tears.

"I know you remember that day. Do you remember what I told you when you wouldn't stop crying?"

Ava nodded: *yes.*

"Right, I told you that when life deals you a bad hand, just play it the best you can. And the very next day you walked into that school, with your brand new yellow back-pack, proud of your new hairdo and everyone loved it. All the other girls got their hair cut short too, just like you. Remember?"

Ava nodded, knowing where the conversation was going.

"Baby, Mrs. Scarborough makes a lot of sense. What's done is done."

Ava looked at her father, pleading for guidance.

"Trust me, I could kill those boys with my bare hands for hurting you the way they did, taking away any chances you got to settle down with a good man. But then your mother's voice just enters my head and tells me I'd just wind up in jail like your Uncle Billy, and then you wouldn't have me or your mother for the rest of your life."

Ava's eyes streamed with tears.

"Pumpkin, this is our only chance to never have to worry about money again. A million dollars is a lot of money if you save it right. Nothing fancy, just keep every-thing normal and that money will go a long way. See, I've got one regular customer and all he does is invest money for rich people. I know he could help me figure this all out. I'll just tell him I won the cash at a slot in Vegas, plus he won't care where I got it anyways. But Ava, this has to be your decision. I'll support you in whatever you decide. I swear it on your mother's soul, I'll do whatever *you* tell me to do. And then we'll never talk about it again."

Ava's bandages darkened with more tears.

"You're all I got left in this world, kiddo." Nick's eyes glistened as he kissed her mummy forehead. "I love you."

Ava struggled to lift her bandaged arms to embrace her father.

Outside in the hallway, Miriam watched Nick and Ava through the interior window. Doctor Morris approached her cautiously.

"Can I help you?"

Miriam returned a cold stare. "No. I was just leaving."

CHAPTER 10

The Verdict

WEDNESDAY, FEBRUARY 6, 1991
6:18 P.M.

In just eleven days, the interior of Wesley's home went from looking like a college co-ed disaster area to a pristine pre-war museum. New gold and sage colored curtains hung in every window. The walls had been carefully re-painted, the antique cherry wood floors had been polished and the broken staircase spindles had been replaced and re-stained. Most noticeably, the old patio furniture had magically disappeared with elegant Scarborough furniture standing in its place. Yet, despite its brand new appearance, the one thing that remained at *Black Acre* was the energy of the house. The dark, eerie feel that was once stale and musty, was now vibrant and bloodthirsty, as if the raping of Ava DeSantis fed the negative energy that possessed it. Yes, somehow the house influenced what had happened that night. And even if it had to wait another century, it looked forward to tasting that blood-filled, carnal debauchery once again.

Wesley, Sebastian and David sat at their new Henry XIII inspired dining room table, unenthusiastically playing poker. Their appearance had become radically different: Wesley, gray-skinned, gaunt and disheveled; Sebastian channeling King Henry XIII himself, fat and slovenly with an invisible red beard; and David, black-eyed, slow and sleepy, still in withdrawal from the party favors he had once adored.

Wesley dealt another hand as the phone rang in the adjacent kitchen.

DINGGG ALING.

They all looked at one another.

"Answer it!" hollered Sebastian.

Wesley darted out of his dark wood mini-throne and answered the wall-mounted corded phone in the kitchen. "Momma?"

All three exchanged looks of heightened stress. This was it. The verdict. The very last moment they would know whether they would continue living well-funded lives or spend the rest of their days sucking the cocks of hardened criminals.

"...And what did he say?" asked Wesley with a broken voice.

Miriam mumbled a long-winded sentence on the other end of the phone line.

"Are you sure?"

Miriam mumbled loudly in return.

"Okay."

Stunned, Wesley just hung up the phone.

Sebastian and David looked at one another, scared beyond measure.

"Well?" asked Sebastian.

"She took the money." Wesley's sad eyes did not match his words.

"Seriously?"

"Yeah, it's done. We're okay."

Sebastian and David erupted with excitement.

"Go Miriam!" yelled Sebastian as he grabbed David and Wesley into a group hug.

"Freedom! Freedom!" yelled David, mimicking William Wallace from *Tales of Scottish Heroes.*

Wesley was silent as his roommates squeezed him roughly, celebrating the greatest victory of their lives. After a while, he broke free from the huddle and quietly pulled away from the celebration. Unnoticed by the others, he walked over to a white upholstered chair in the living room and plopped down, exhausted.

Sebastian and David continued celebrating in the kitchen. First they pulled out bags of chips and jars of dip from the pantry. Then they moved to the refrigerator, yanking out a vintage bottle of Dom Pérignon they were saving for graduation.

"Open that hooker!" said Sebastian in a rare, jovial tone.

Meanwhile in the living room, Wesley was alone in his new white chair, with his golden-fleeced head of hair buried in his hands, not uttering a single celebratory word.

Instead, Wesley was quietly crying to himself.

Ava...

CHAPTER 11

15 YEARS, 7 MONTHS & 28 DAYS LATER

WEDNESDAY, OCTOBER 4, 2006
10:13 A.M

A stiff, elderly Southern lawyer sat at an opulent desk, reading a teleprompter like a Disney animatronic. "Have you been injured? Has someone done you wrong? If so, call the law offices of Hall, Wentworth and Garcia."

"Cut!" yelled Wesley Scarborough, looking upon the commercial shoot with disgust. Now thirty-six, Wesley was more mature and handsome than ever, dressed in a navy blue power suit adorned with a bright orange silk tie. His formerly long, wavy blonde hair was now darker and slicked back with hair gel, his eyes were as bright blue as ever, and his yellow-gold wedding band beamed against the color of his just-vacationed-in-Aruba tan skin.

"Let's try this again!" he shouted.

Lilly Torres, Wesley's pint-sized Latina firecracker assistant, quickly approached him on the set. "This isn't working," she whispered into his ear.

"No shit. What about Garcia?"

A charismatic Hispanic man in his forties sat off to the side, observing their conversation.

Lilly furiously shook her head. "No, no, no, you'll alienate the natives. What if you get mister corpse here to do it from memory? Or maybe we can ask—?"

Wesley's vibrating cell phone interrupted her.

"You better get that. Could be the big call."

"Give me two seconds." Wesley took several steps away from the set, pulled the cell phone from his belt loop clip and answered it. "Hey, honey. How are you feeling?"

"No baby yet, so stop worrying," said his wife cheerfully on the other end.

"Good 'cause I'm in the middle of directing a commercial. Can I call you back in thirty?"

"Well, I just need a few seconds really. I need to ask you something important."

He looked out to the crowd of people around him. "Okay, let's take a ten minute break everybody! Be back here at ten-thirty!" Wesley then turned back into the phone. "Okay, Michelle. Shoot."

Twenty-seven-year-old Michelle Scarborough was the kind of peppy Southern Belle that would constantly re-enact her High School Prom Queen speech in the mirror when nobody was looking. Her small frame, alabaster skin, shoulder-length fluffy brown hair and baby-doll brown eyes perfectly complimented Wesley's golden Adonis features. She stood eight-and-a-half months pregnant in the living room of their brand new home in Buckhead, surrounded by a crew of immigrant workers industriously unpacking stacks of moving boxes behind her. Sitting close by at a round kitchen table was Miriam Scarborough (who magically hadn't aged one bit) and a flamboyantly dressed man with books of wallpaper swatches before him.

"I hate to bother you at work, Wes, but we need you to cast the deciding vote. Fish or trains?"

Wesley was instantly annoyed. "What kind of fish?"

She looked at the man sitting at the table. He held up two samples of colorful fish wallpaper. "Tropical fish."

"Tropical is fine."

"Wes, really think about it."

Miriam rose from the table and approached Michelle.

"Tropical. River. Whatever you like, baby. It's your choice," replied Wesley.

"Let me talk to him." Miriam gently pulled the phone from Michelle's hand.

"Oh, here's your mother…" Michelle's eyes fell to the floor as she handed the cordless handset to Miriam.

"Wesley, you should *at least* have the decency to put some serious thought into this. In fact, you should have made these decisions months ago! Your baby is due in less than two weeks and you haven't even assembled the crib yet. You're not going to be able to work eighty hours a week when the baby gets here. Do you hear me?"

Wesley was five years old again. "Yes, ma'am."

"Good. Now do you prefer the fish or the trains?"

"What does Michelle want?"

"She likes the fish. However, I think trains are more masculine and will be more practical as your son grows older."

"Trains sound good."

"That's what I thought. Trains it is then." Miriam transitioned from defense lawyer back into mother mode. "Okay, I know you're busy at work, sugar, so I'll let you go. Have a good day."

"You too, bye." Wesley hung up the phone and rolled his eyes at Lilly.

"Grandzilla?"

"What do you think?"

Lilly smirked. "You lead a charmed life, my dear."

"And you will too if you find a way to reanimate this corpse so we can get back to the office."

"I'll do my best, captain." Lilly quickly walked back over to the set and pulled the old robot lawyer aside.

Wesley ran his hand through his hair. *Please God, let this day get better…'cause I'm ready to blow my fucking stack if it doesn't.*

CHAPTER 12

TOO CLOSE TO HOME

WEDNESDAY, OCTOBER 4, 2006
12:11 P.M.

The shiny steel elevator doors flashed open. Wesley and Lilly, alone in the elevator, exited right in front of a steel and glass receptionist desk that sat below a sign that read: SCARCOM – Scarborough Public Relations.

Everything about this fucking place vomited *success*. The floor was made of custom black Berber carpet; the large panoramic city view windows were framed by burgundy suede drapes; and the entire space was honeycombed with dozens of glass cubicles occupied by worker-bee Ivy League graduates. In fact, there were so many beautiful people in glass cages at ScarCom that it resembled a high-end puppy store showcasing its best of inbred dogs.

One of those inbred dogs was a beautiful blonde receptionist who quietly moonlighted as a librarian in porn videos. She handed Lilly a stack of messages as they both walked by. "Good afternoon, Mr. Scarborough. Miss Torres."

"Good afternoon, Lola."

Wesley picked up a large stack of mail from the counter. "Has FedEx delivered yet?"

The receptionist served her bodacious tits on the steel desk as she spoke: "No, Mr. Scarborough. FedEx usually *comes* around one o'clock."

Wesley was immune to her innuendos at this point. In fact, Wesley was so accustomed to beautiful women trying to get on his second wife waiting list that he didn't even acknowledge their existence. "Just buzz me when he arrives, Lola. Thanks."

———⊗≫∞———

Wesley and Lilly walked diligently towards a huge glass office occupying the entire end of the long hallway. Naturally, as Owner/President/CEO of the company, Wesley had picked the best office for himself.

"Warner, Davidson, Weinstein, Blah, Blah, Blah, called to see if you're available Thursday morning for a pitch meeting," said Lilly in one fast-paced breath as she read the phone messages aloud.

"Am I available?"

"No. But I hear they're shopping for a new PR firm. The Jenkins trial is coming up in December."

"The doctor who drowned his wife?"

"Yes, the doctor who *allegedly* drowned his wife."

"Okay, *allegedly* set up the meeting then."

They finally arrived at his ridiculous office. It had a complete floor-to-ceiling clear-day view of downtown Atlanta, and a fully stocked black marble wet bar to the right.

"What else?" Wesley tossed his mail onto the spotless, stainless steel desk.

"I'm heading out for lunch. Do you want steak or chicken today?"

"No, nothing for me, thanks." Wesley sat down in his oversized black leather throne.

Lilly gave him a suspicious look. "No lunch?"

"I had a big breakfast."

"Suit yourself." Lilly turned to exit. "You know, starving won't help you look any better naked."

Wesley chuckled. "Watch it, Lilly. People might misconstrue our relationship."

"Please. Everyone here knows I like meat on my bones."

He smiled. "Just go eat."

Lilly giggled as she exited the office. Four seconds later, she returned with her black eyes wide open. "Mr. Holt is here to see you."

Wesley quickly stood at attention. "Daniel?"

Daniel Holt, a six-foot-five, silver-haired Texan wearing a white cowboy hat and a black suit entered the office. He was the sort of double-digit millionaire lawyer that drove a ten-year old Ford pickup truck and ordered custom Armani suits to match his favorite shotguns.

"Daniel. What a surprise?"

Lilly quickly exited the office and closed the door.

"How are you, Wesley?"

They shook hands.

"I'm doing well, thank you. I'm just surprised my receptionist didn't announce your arrival."

"She was busy flirtin' with the FedEx kid so I walked on by. I hope you don't mind."

"Of course not, you can visit any time. Please. Have a seat." Wesley flashed his charming smile as Daniel sat down in one of two burgundy client chairs, crossing his long perfectly tailored legs in the process.

"So how are you feeling these days?" asked Wesley.

"Fair to middlin', thank you. The cancer is still in remission, so that's something to be grateful about."

"Yes, sir, very grateful."

"Indeed."

"Well, it's always good to see you, Daniel. Unless we screwed something up, of course." Wesley let out a nervous chuckle. "Can I get you a drink? Whiskey? Or is it bourbon?"

"No, son, still tryin' to cut down before five. Got orders from the General."

"Understood."

Daniel eyeballed a picture of Michelle in her wedding gown on the desk. "Speaking of generals, is your son here yet?"

"No, only two more weeks. Thank goodness too. Things are crazy at home."

Daniel belted out a huge belly laugh. "Son, if you think things are crazy at home now just wait until that baby comes. Trust me. It only goes downhill from here."

Wesley dove straight back into business. "You know, Daniel, it's not your style to just drop in without having your assistant confirm our appointment at least three times. Are you sure everything is all right?"

Daniel's face changed. "Well, that I don't know yet, Wesley...I have a very sensitive situation I need to make you aware of. That's why I'm here."

"Okay. Shoot."

Daniel's loud Texan voice now barely spoke above a whisper. "Do you remember me tellin' you, around two months ago, about a woman who filed a sexual harassment claim against one of our partners, Jacob Saffroy?"

"The paralegal, right?"

"Yes, that's the one. What you may or may not be aware of is that we found it in our budget to give her a *generous* bonus to stay with our firm."

"Yes, I am aware of it."

Daniel leaned in closer and lowered his voice further. "Well, things have gone horribly wrong, Wes. Is it safe to speak in here?"

Wesley had never seen such concern on Daniel's face before. He was a world-renowned trial attorney that had struck God's fear into thousands of jurors over three decades. *What could possibly scare him this badly?* "Sure, Daniel. Go ahead."

"Well, yesterday afternoon, the girl arranged a secret meeting with our HR director. She claimed that Jake forced himself on her while they were working late the night before."

"What do you mean by *forced himself*?" Just as soon as the question left his mouth, Wesley realized he did not want to hear the answer.

"Wesley, the girl claims that Jake raped her...in the supply room."

Rape? Wesley tried to mask his reaction. "I wouldn't worry about it too much, Daniel. It's just her word against his. I mean, how do you know she's not trying to get more money out of you?"

Daniel pulled a small black thumb drive out of his interior breast pocket and placed it on the steel desk. Fear quickly filled his eyes. "I installed a hidden video camera in the supply room last month to catch folks stealin' office supplies."

Wesley's stomach filled with dread.

"I saw it, Wes. I saw the whole thing with my own eyes."

Wesley was quietly horrified. In his thirteen years as a public relations specialist, he had never encountered a case of rape before. Obviously, the situation hit way too close to home.

"How clear is the tape?"

"Crystal clear. And it's terrible. Just terrible."

"Is there any possibility that this was consensual?"

"None whatsoever. She cried out for help the entire time. Especially at the beginning while he was beating her."

Wesley's stomach dropped another foot with that comment. "Has anyone else seen this?"

"No. Just me. I came right over just as soon as I reviewed the footage in my office."

Wesley drew a long, deep breath, knowing he was taking a risk by making the following suggestion: "Daniel, you have to go to the police with this."

"Police? You must be crazy, son!" Wesley prepared for the worst. "This security tape will destroy our entire firm! It will destroy *my reputation* once and for all!"

"I understand, Daniel, but this is serious. I'm just your spokesperson. I'm not a lawyer."

Daniel grinded his lips together. "I have enough goddamn lawyers as it is, Wes. I need *your* help. I need you to protect me if this gets out."

Wesley struggled to find the right words. "I don't know if I'm the right person for this situation."

"That's nonsense. No one in this town can handle a crisis better than you, Wes. You were the only person willing *to even try* to save my career after that third DUI. And you pulled it off. I'll always be indebted to you for that."

"Thank you, Daniel, but this one…this case is a little different."

"Bullshit." Daniel sharpened his steel gray eyes. "No one is better than you. And you know it."

Wesley always knew that his stellar record of defending the city's most prominent attorneys in the court of public opinion would one day turn on him. He didn't know how. He didn't know when. He just knew that one day he would be asked to perform a miracle impossible to accomplish, and then burn at the stake for failing to deliver. "Okay, I'll see what I can do about it."

"Now, what do you need from me?"

Wesley was flustered, even resentful. "Email me her full name, HR records, work history, resume—"

The intercom BUZZED loudly. Wesley pressed the speaker button on the phone.

"I'm in a very important meeting, Lola. I'll be out in twenty minutes."

"I'm sorry to interrupt, Mr. Scarborough, but Sebastian's mother-in-law is on line three."

Wesley was perplexed. "Dorothy?"

"Yes. She said it was an emergency."

The baby? "Please excuse me, Daniel."

"No, of course."

Wesley picked up the handset. "Hello, Dorothy? What's going on?"

Dorothy spoke on the other line for a long minute as Wesley's golden face turned expressionless.

"But I just talked to him last night…"

Daniel gathered himself. "I'll let you go, Wes. Sounds important."

Wesley spoke like a zombie into the handset. "Okay, I'll be right over." He hung up the phone, speechless.

Daniel stood up, ready to leave. "You're pale as a ghost, son. I'm afraid to ask."

"They found my best friend this morning in the basement of a sex club. He's dead."

"Christ, Wesley. I'm very sorry to hear that. This can definitely wait."

"Do you mind, Daniel? I really need to see his wife."

"Don't even think about it. Please. Go."

Wesley stood up and moved towards the door. Daniel picked up the flash drive from the steel desk. "What should I do with this?"

"Destroy it. It's too risky."

Daniel moved closer to Wesley at the door, "But it's the only guarantee we have that Jake won't turn against us if the shit hits the fan."

Wesley nodded as if he had a point.

"Never trust a cornered rat."

"You're right. It will be safer with me." Wesley grabbed the flash drive from Daniel's hand, walked back over to his desk, placed it in the top drawer and locked it with a small key. "We'll figure out what to do with it tomorrow."

"Thanks, Wes. Let me walk you to the elevator. I'm heading out that way anyway."

CHAPTER 13

UGLIER HOMES AND GARDENS

WEDNESDAY, OCTOBER 4, 2006
1:43 P.M.

Wesley stood on the doorstep of an ugly, no truly *hideous*, six thousand-square-foot brick home in Druid Hills. Ironically, the gargantuan thick-trunked trees that flooded the property were the prettiest in the neighborhood, carefully discarding leaves of red, orange and yellow like an old vaudeville stripper teasing an audience waiting for the big reveal.

Dorothy Windham, a sixty-five-year-old Tennessee blue-hair, came to the repulsive burnt orange front door to greet Wesley.

"Hey, Dorothy. I am so sorry."

"Please come in. Susie is waiting for you."

Wesley entered the home. As he walked through the mismatched yellow and mauve foyer, he saw random somber people scattered around the living room. *These must be the neighbors*, he thought to himself. He then spotted

Sebastian's two youngest asshole children – fat and red-haired like their father – playing with toys gleefully on the floor.

"Where's Susie?"

Dorothy pursed her lips. "She's in her bedroom crying. I told her not to speak to anyone until she talks to you first."

Dorothy led Wesley down a hallway of black and white family photos, towards a set of hunter green double doors. Dorothy knocked on the door harshly. "Wesley's here, Susie. Open up."

Sebastian's distraught wife, thirty-five-year-old Susie O'Connor, opened the door. She was a woman so plain, so verbally abused and so invisible, she doesn't even deserve a character description.

As the door opened, Susie grabbed Wesley and hugged him for dear life. "Wesley!" she cried aloud.

He hugged her back with all of his might. "We'll figure this out, Susie." His bright blue eyes welled with tears. "I'll help you and the kids out of this. I promise."

In the bedroom, Wesley rubbed Susie's back as they sat together on the patchwork quilt bedspread. Dorothy leaned against the dresser with her arms crossed, not sheading a single tear.

"But why would he choke himself in the first place?" asked Wesley.

Dorothy cleared her tar-lined throat. "The police said he was performing something called," she pulled a piece of white paper from the top of the dresser, "auto-erotic asphyxiation, whatever the hell that is."

"I don't understand."

"Apparently, it's common for men at this place to sneak downstairs and do this to themselves. And if a person goes too far, they can die from it."

Susie cried aloud.

Dorothy hacked phlegm for a few moments, then continued. "Wesley, the kids can't find out their daddy died this way. We need a story."

Wesley immediately snapped into spin cycle. "Just tell everyone Sebastian went there to entertain a wealthy client from out of town…and while Sebastian was at the club, he suddenly felt very ill, quietly slipped into the bathroom and collapsed. He died of a heart attack on the spot."

"And how do we explain why he was entertaining clients at a sex club?" snarled Dorothy. "This shit story ain't gonna fly too well with my church family."

"Well, you can explain to everyone at church that it was *his client* who insisted they go there. He was from... Japan. You know how kinky Japanese men can be."

"No, I don't. But as much as Sebastian hated foreigners, that would be exactly the sort of thing he would say."

"Exactly."

Susie shot a look at her mother, then started crying again.

"All right, that's the story."

"Good. I'll make sure my team cleans up the police blotters and then we'll write a glowing obituary. I'll get it in tomorrow."

"Thank you, Wesley. I can't tell you how much we appreciate this."

"It's the least I can do, Dorothy."

"But we have an even bigger problem with the insurance company." Dorothy struggled to catch a full breath. "We're gonna need your help to find a good lawyer."

Insurance company? Sebastian hadn't even been dead twenty-four hours and his mother-in-law already had an answer from his life insurance company. Talk about quick service.

"So are they refusing to pay because it was self-inflicted?"

"Oh, no, they'll pay out the money…to the beneficiary listed on the policy."

Susie howled with pain.

"What? Susie is not on the policy?"

"Not anymore."

"I don't understand."

"Apparently, Sebastian mailed in a change of beneficiary form last month. They said the signature matches and it was notarized so there's nothing we can do about it."

"Why would he do that? He loved Susie and the kids."

Susie howled again.

"Who the hell knows? Why would he stick a dog collar around his neck and jerk himself off to death?"

Susie cried aloud, "Momma!"

"How can you cry for that man after what he did to you?"

Susie cried louder.

"Dorothy, who's the new beneficiary?"

"He left you and the kids *with nothing!*"

"Dorothy—"

"I'll never forgive his fat ass!"

"Dorothy! Who gets the money?" commanded Wesley.

The room was silent.

"The National Democratic Party."

Wesley was paralyzed with shock. "What?"

Susie began screaming violently: "That fucking bastard left them five million dollars!!!" She continued to howl, crying hysterically.

"That's impossible." Wesley's voice was almost imperceptible.

"That's what I thought too. But it's true." Dorothy's yellowing eyes finally revealed how sad she was for her family.

"I'll find you a lawyer. Today."

Back at the front door, Dorothy followed Wesley outside to the front porch.

"Oh, and can you call your mutual friends and let them know the funeral is on Saturday? Buckhead Baptist Church. The service starts at ten in the morning."

"Sure. I think I still have everyone's number."

"And what about your old college roommate? The slow one. I forgot his name."

"Oh, David. David Reilly. We lost touch, I don't know, around six or seven years ago, but I'll try to find him. Anyone else?"

"Just whoever you think should be there. But don't invite any of his whores on the side. There's only enough room for 500 people."

Dorothy shot Wesley a look.

"Just hang in there, Dorothy. We'll all get through this...somehow."

CHAPTER 14

Finding David Reilly

WEDNESDAY, OCTOBER 4, 2006
9:12 P.M.

Wesley sat at his brand new kitchen table in front of a laptop computer, talking on the phone. Sitting immediately next to him was his wife, Michelle, so disgustingly cute and pregnant, dressed in adult size footed duck pajamas. She was holding a purple magic marker in one hand, and a list of crossed out phone numbers in the other…

Only one phone number remained on the list.

"Hello. May I speak to David Reilly?…Hi, David this is Wes Scarborough from Anniston University. Do I have the right David Reilly?…No problem, sir…Have a good night."

Wesley hung up the black cordless phone as Michelle crossed off the last number on her list. She gave Wesley an endearing look that said, *at least you tried*. After a long bit of silence, tears started to stream down Wesley's exhausted face.

Michelle moved in closer and hugged Wesley as he cried like a little boy in her arms.

CHAPTER 15

My Big Fat Southern Funeral

SATURDAY, OCTOBER 7, 2006
12:58 P.M.

Yes, the interior of the O'Connor house was so repulsive, it looked as if it had been decorated by two straight men on a dare. The mauve and seafoam green Miami Vice era furniture was now filled with large black blobs of people in mourning…socializing and exchanging business cards now that Sebastian's mega-rich investor clients were up for grabs.

All three of Susie's flame-haired, chubby children were horsing around on the stained living room floor while the TV played *Sponge Bob* on Nickelodeon. Wesley and the very pregnant Michelle stood in the living room near the television, chatting with the invisible widow.

"No, the music was perfect. The whole service was excellent. You did a wonderful job," shared Wesley.

"Thank you, but my mother gets all the credit. I don't know what I would've done without her help." Susie's eyes fell to the floor.

"I completely understand. My momma is everything to me too." Michelle's kind eyes responded in a way that showed how much she genuinely felt Susie's pain. In her mind, losing Wesley was her greatest fear of all time.

"I just wish she could help me wake up from this nightmare," said Susie.

"I know. We feel exactly the same way."

Just then, Susie's youngest child grabbed the remote control and started flipping the channels. The other two siblings fought hard to get it back.

"Give it to me!"

"I want Sponge Bob!"

During the fight, the TV landed on a local news station. On the screen, a young black anchorwoman spoke while the words *Breaking News* scrolled across the top…

"Jacob Saffroy, a partner at the prestigious law firm of Holt, Weil, Richardson and Saffroy…"

Wesley immediately turned his attention to the TV.

"…has just been arrested by the Atlanta police moments ago."

The television showed a live image of an attractive dark-haired man being led out of an office building in handcuffs.

"Sources say that an unidentified woman, who is an employee of the firm, claims that Saffroy raped her while they were working late last Monday night..."

Wesley's cell phone rang. He answered it abruptly.

"I'm leaving right now."

CHAPTER 16

THE SCARCOM GANG

MONDAY, OCTOBER 9, 2006
8:03 A.M.

Wesley, Lilly and eight other staff members (affection-ately known around the office as the ScarCom Gang) sat at a spaceship sized steel conference table, wearing the same smelly clothes as the day before. A large, steaming double necked coffee thermos and two brand new boxes of donuts sat in the middle of the table, teasing everyone who was starving in the room.

Wesley cleared his throat. "Let's go ahead and get started. What do we have?"

A young bi-racial woman with natural, bushy hair spoke up. "Sarah Elizabeth Vinson is a twenty-six-year-old divorced mother of three. She enjoys riding horses, mainly because she was born on a horse farm in Louisville, Kentucky—"

"I'm not writing a fucking *Biography* episode, Dierdra. Give me what I need."

Dierdra straightened up in her chair. "Miss Vinson was a stripper at the Emerald Club before it was shut down."

"Really? And you confirmed that?"

A thin man in a lime green sweater chimed in. "Yes, we did. Dierdra and I visited one of her co-workers last night. She said that everyone who worked at the Emerald Club knew Sarah offered more than just lap dances for a living."

"Which means *what* exactly?"

The gang was taken aback. Wesley wasn't usually this condescending.

"Sarah Vinson was a prostitute."

"And you base this on one person's allegation? That's weak, Ed. Not enough."

Before he could respond, a middle-aged black woman in a purple power-suit interrupted. "Well, I have her mug shots right here." The woman tossed two full size police photos across the table. "She was arrested twice for solicitation. Once in 2001 and again in 2003."

Wesley picked up the photos, examining each one closely. "That's only three years ago." But just as the words came out of his mouth, his heart sunk. He knew without a doubt that Sarah Vinson was an innocent victim of a brutal attack. But now a lethal mistake in her past would make it that much easier for him to destroy her. And like a hired soldier paid to kill the enemy – without any regard for their guilt or innocence – Wesley had to finish off Sarah Vinson, without any regard for the individual cost to his soul.

"Is the co-worker you visited willing to sign an affidavit?" asked Wesley.

Dierdra replied. "Unfortunately, no. Reason is, she respects Sarah too much for cleaning up her act and going back to school to become a paralegal."

Wesley felt a pang of guilt. Despite his discomfort, he proceeded with his mission. "Dierdra. Ed. I need you both to leak the co-worker's name to the press. They'll make her talk."

"Will do."

"Anything else?"

A young, heavy-set man with black-rimmed glasses raised his hand.

"Yes, Derek."

"Maybe we can find someone who paid Sarah for sex? Like one of the NBA players who got busted there a few years back?"

"We'll need more time for that," added Ed.

"And why would an NBA player publically admit to such a thing?" asked Dierdra.

"Perhaps a lifetime of free legal counsel would be an incentive?" replied Derek.

"That's a good idea. Get on it," added Wesley.

A meek Indian woman in the back of the room raised her hand. "Wait. How much time do we have, Wes?"

Wesley looked at his Rolex. "I'm scheduling a press conference just as soon as Saffroy posts bail, so that means y'all have...six hours."

The crowd reacted, *that's not enough time.*

"Good. Let's get to work."

The entire group rose from the table, preparing to exit the conference room. Derek grabbed a fresh box of donuts; Dierdra poured herself a small vat of black coffee.

Wesley quietly pulled Ed aside. "I need you to find an old college buddy of mine. It's important." He handed him a yellow post it with writing on it.

"No problem. I'll get right on it, sir."

CHAPTER 17

LIGHTS, CAMERA, FICTION!

MONDAY, OCTOBER 9, 2006
2:37 P.M.

The Blue Room at the Ritz Carlton was packed with TV camera crews and newspaper reporters. Wesley stood center stage on the podium, with Daniel Holt immediately by his side. Dressed like twins, they looked dapper in their Conservanazi power uniforms of navy blue business suits, crisp white shirts and matching bull red ties.

Wesley pointed into the audience. "Yes, you."

A petite brunette reporter from the third row stood up. "Mr. Scarborough, is it true that your clients were fully aware of the problems between the unidentified employee and Mr. Saffroy?"

"Yes, my clients were aware of unsubstantiated rumors that the two were romantically involved, but naturally, that does not warrant an official investigation into the personal lives of two consenting adults."

Wesley flashed his multi-million-dollar smile.

The female reporter beamed right back at him. "Thank you."

A flock of hands rocketed back into the air.

"Yes. You." Wesley pointed to a short African-American man in the back row.

"I understand that the unidentified employee is actually Sarah Elizabeth Vinson, a former stripper who worked at the Emerald Club." The audience faked a gasp of surprise. "Is this true?"

"It is not my place to confirm or deny the identity of the accuser, Mr. Johnson. It is up to her as to whether or not she wishes to reveal her identity to the public. Next question."

A buffed bald man with glasses rose from the left corner. "Mr. Scarborough, another exotic dancer who worked with Sarah Vinson at the Emerald Club claims that Sarah was a prostitute before joining the firm. Were any of your clients aware of this?"

"Again, it is not my place to share information about an employee's past. You will have to wait to speak to the accuser should she decide to reveal her identity in public. Next question."

Wesley pointed to a delicate Asian lady wearing a red sweater in the front row.

"Mr. Scarborough, now that her name has been used, I might as well use it too…"

The audience erupted in laughter.

"Sarah Vinson told a close friend of hers that she received a large bonus from the firm two months ago to withdraw a sexual harassment claim. How do you respond to this?"

"It is true that my clients gave the unidentified employee a bonus for her outstanding work several months ago. In fact, a large percentage of employees at Holt, Weil, Richardson and Saffroy receive bonuses for work well done. However, it is important to stress that my clients had no knowledge whatsoever of the accuser's intention to file any type of claim against the firm. Next question."

An older man with a deep-toned radio voice rose from his seat. "Mr. Scarborough, do the other partners fully back Mr. Saffroy in this matter?"

"My clients have absolutely no reason to deny Jacob Saffroy his absolute right of remaining innocent until proven otherwise. Therefore, he will remain a senior partner throughout this matter and will continue to conduct business as usual."

"What about Miss Vinson? Does she still have a job?"

The reporters laughed.

"The unidentified employee is again, quite valuable at the firm and has an open invitation to resume her duties whenever she wishes to. Next question."

"Mr. Scarborough, do you think Jacob Saffroy is guilty?"

Wesley hesitated. "This is a matter for the police to resolve, and in the meantime, my clients will continue to serve their clients with impeccable legal counsel as they have for the past fifty-seven years—"

A male reporter interrupted. "But Mr. Scarborough, *aren't you* a rapist?"

Time froze.

There standing in the middle of the sea of reporters was Ava DeSantis – naked, bloodied and battered – smiling like the Devil waiting for good news.

Wesley's heart pumped out of his chest. His ears were ringing with fright.

"Excuse me?"

The male reporter repeated his question. "I asked if you thought he was a rapist."

Evil Ava grinned a wide toothless smile.

Wesley mustered everything he had to answer. "I have no reason to believe the accusations made against me, nor do my clients. There is no concrete evidence to support this very serious allegation."

Daniel shot Wesley a serious look of concern. "Let's wrap this up."

Wesley blinked his eyes hard. Suddenly, Ava disappeared from the audience. After a few long seconds, the room was confused by Wesley's silence.

Daniel stepped up to the podium. "We will keep y'all posted as additional information develops. Thank you, thank you all for your time."

The reporters reacted, they obviously wanted more.

Wesley exited the podium and walked backstage. Daniel Holt followed him.

"Great job there, son," Daniel patted Wesley on the shoulder. "I especially liked how you made it personal by saying 'accusations against me'"

"I did?"

"Just shows the press how much you take our defense to heart. That's why we hired you, son. You're the best crisis man in town."

Wesley's knees suddenly became weak.

Daniel held the exit door for Wesley. "Now let's go grab a few cocktails at the lobby bar before the General notices I'm missing."

Wesley faked a pleasant smile. They walked out of the dark backstage area and into the light of the glittering Ritz Carlton lobby.

CHAPTER 18

KILL THE MESSENGER

MONDAY, OCTOBER 9, 2006
4:57 P.M.

Wesley drove his brand new black Cadillac Escalade through the city's busy streets, relieved to be finished with the stress of such a career-making (or breaking) press conference. It was already rush hour (or death hour as Wesley liked to call it), a time where Atlanta traffic seemed to have no mercy on its vehicular prisoners, or provide any rhyme or reason as to why two million people had to be on the road at the exact same moment in time.

Wesley's monster vehicle featured a top of the line, in-dash computer system with a voice activated phone system. And when I-285 turned into a parking lot, Wesley would scream at the little person who lived in his SUV for not reminding him to take an alternate route.

"Call Lilly," he said to the computer genie inside the dashboard.

"Calling Lilly Torres..." replied the female computer voice.

After two short rings, the line picked up on the other end: "Boy, if you're half as good in bed as you are on TV, then I'm a jealous girl."

Lilly's loud voice echoed over the speakers.

"Now what if Michelle was in the car with me? You could get me into serious trouble saying shit like that."

"Please. Everyone knows I'm not your type otherwise you would've slept with me a *long* time ago."

Wesley laughed. "I'm not that bad…anymore."

"A leopard never changes his spots. Or in your case, an elephant never forgets he has a big trunk."

Wesley laughed out loud.

"Anyway, the phone is ringing off the hook. Are you on your way in?"

Wesley was pleased to see traffic was finally moving at a solid forty miles an hour. "No, I'm heading home to take a nap. But I'll be back in the office after dinner."

"Will you remember to visit Michelle?"

"Yes, I will visit my wife. Thank you for reminding me, Lilly."

"Okay then. Let me get your phone messages…Oh, and your father called to remind you about dinner tomorrow night at their place. Six o'clock sharp."

"Shit. I forgot about that. What else did he say?"

"He said that he doesn't forgive you for taking after your mother in becoming the world's greatest liar on TV today."

"Figures."

"I'm joking, Wes! Lighten up. He just asked me to remind you about dinner."

Wesley was not amused. His father often made snide comments about how he turned out to be just like his mother. "Okay. What else?"

"Clark Wright wants to interview you for an article on how businesses can fight bogus sexual harassment claims."

"Sounds good. Set that up."

"And Barbara from Channel Five wants an interview with Daniel Holt for the eleven o'clock broadcast. I already set that up with him…"

Wesley cautiously approached an intersection.

"Good. What time is the briefing?"

"Nine thirty…Also, Ava DeSantis called. She said she needs to meet with you as soon as possible."

Wesley was dumbfounded.

He ran the red light.

A large, Italian bakery truck driver SCREECHED his tires as he approached the Escalade, gliding through the intersection like a duck on water. Wesley looked into the driver's squinted face as he skidded towards him, sweating from his brow…

CLACK!

The truck tapped Wesley's driver's side door, barely making a dent.

"Ay dios mio! What was that? Are you all right?"

Wesley was in shock. He could barely catch his breath.

"Wesley! Are you okay? Talk to me!"

Wesley continued to breathe heavily. "I'm okay. I'm okay."

"Jesus Christ, you've got be more careful driving! You have a baby on the way!"

"Fuck, Lilly. I know that."

"You damn near gave me a heart attack. What the hell happened?"

"Don't worry about it."

Wesley saluted the truck driver and continued driving.

The truck driver sighed back in relief, grateful he wouldn't be losing his job for hitting yet another vehicle.

Wesley brushed off the incident quickly. It was nothing in comparison to what Lilly just dumped upon him. "Give me that last message again."

"Are you crazy? I'm getting off this phone."

"Lilly. Read the message to me again."

"I don't even remember which one I was on…"

Wesley was incredulous. "Did you say Ava DeSantis called or was that my imagination?"

"Oh, yes. I spoke to her myself."

Wesley's chiseled face turned to stone.

"Here it is… She said she needs to meet with you right away and that you would know what it's about."

Wesley tried to hide his concern. "Did she leave a number?"

"Yes, do you need it now?"

"No, no. I'll get it later. Just leave it on my desk."

"I will. And you have about a dozen more messages, but I'm getting off this goddamn phone before you kill yourself. I'll see you at the office later tonight."

Wesley wanted to get home faster than ever. "Okay, Lilly. Thanks."

Wesley turned onto Birchwood Road, a gorgeous oak-lined street in the prestigious neighborhood of Buckhead. The sun was drifting down and the wind was blowing gently, ushering colorful leaves across the road in front of him. He drove three hundred yards then pulled into the circular driveway of a large, brown Tudor style home. It was the kind of large single family home packed closely together with other large single family homes that one often finds in *kill me now it's so fucking Beaver Cleaver* upper-crust Atlanta neighborhoods.

Wesley parked the Escalade in the tan stone driveway, but he did not exit the vehicle. Instead, he sat in the driver's seat, quietly meditating for a solid five minutes. His goal? Regain his composure before facing his wife. Because no matter what happens to him over the next several weeks, or months, or years, *Michelle can never find out about Ava.*

Yes, Wesley finally realized how much he would lose if the truth ever came out about Jacob Saffroy...or the crime *he* committed fifteen years ago.

Jesus Christ. What have I done?

<hr />

Wesley opened the front door of his new home with an unfamiliar gleaming silver key. As soon as he entered, his senses were assaulted by the smell of new paint and the visual of pristine, fluffy white living room furniture surrounded by dirty cardboard boxes. He carefully placed his briefcase on the faux-ivory foyer table before him, unsure of what the house rules were yet.

"Baby! You're home!"

Michelle, wearing a pink Juicy Couture velvet jump suit, erupted from the sofa and waddled to the front door. She threw her arms around Wesley, hugging him tightly. "Baby, you were fantastic today. I'm so proud of you!" she exclaimed in her native South Georgia twang.

Wesley looked into Michelle's innocent, baby girl brown eyes, and then gave her a long, sexy, French kiss.

"What was that for?"

"For making me a better person."

Michelle grinned. "I think you need some sleep, honey. You're getting delusional."

Wesley partially smiled back. Seconds later, he became emotional. "I was just thinking about us in the driveway, Michelle, and you know, ever since I met you, my whole outlook on life changed. You make me want to become a better man. For you and the baby. I just want to forget about all of this bullshit and start a whole new life. Something real, something wholesome, just the three of us." He bent down and lightly pressed his cheek against her huge belly. "Y'all mean the world to me."

Michelle squinted her eyes, not entirely convinced of Wesley's sincerity. "What happened to you today? Did you read somewhere that pregnant women need to be sweet talked like this or—?"

Wesley interrupted her question with another long, passionate kiss. But this time, Wesley *wanted* his beautiful wife. He moved his hand to caress her bouncy brown hair...then down her back...over her small, tight ass... pulling gently on the back of her waistband, signaling that he wanted her to take those off.

"Stop, honey. Please."

Wesley ignored Michelle's words and continued pulling down her pink velvet sweatpants as he kissed her.

She sharply pulled away. "I told you. I'm not in the mood."

"Come on, Michelle."

"What? I don't get a say?" Her tone quickly turned dark.

"Michelle, it's been almost *three* months. There's only so much hand lotion a married man can take."

"You're disgusting!" Michelle marched back into the living room.

"Come on." Wesley followed her.

"Well, why don't I let *you* carry the baby for a while and we'll see how much you feel like having sex!" She continued marching through the living room, down the hallway and into the master suite, slamming the door behind her.

"Shit. Michelle? Open the door."

Silence.

"Come on Michelle? You're acting childish."

CLICK. The door was locked.

Wesley threw a fit, punching the air around him. "Shit! Shit! Shit!"

Afterwards, he moped back to the living room, threw himself onto the fluffy white sofa and kicked his dirty dress shoes on the armrest...

When he finally settled down, he passed out for twelve solid hours...

Swearing in his dreams like a sailor, with a matching angry scowl on his sea-worn beautiful face.

CHAPTER 19

The Spin Machine

TUESDAY, OCTOBER 10, 2006
8:17 A.M.

The ScarCom Gang squirmed around the spaceship conference room table, waiting for Wesley to arrive.

"Should we start?" asked Dierdra, wearing brightly colored pumpkin earrings and a brown fuzzy sweater to match her free-spirited hair.

"No, give him a few more minutes," replied Lilly, looking sharper than ever in a sleek black shift dress. "He should be here any second."

Just as Lilly spoke, Wesley entered the room looking haggard and wearing the same Conservanazi ensemble from the day before. Lilly quietly pulled Wesley aside. "What the hell happened to you last night? I waited here for five hours," she whispered.

"Don't fuck with me today" he said in a full volume voice.

"Ouch."

The porn librarian receptionist popped her head in the room. "You needed something, sir?"

"Coffee," commanded Wesley.

"Yes, sir. Right away."

He then turned back to Lilly. "Where are those messages from yesterday?"

"I put them on your desk. Like you told me to do last—"

"Go get them."

Lilly had no idea what was going on, but she knew that it was best to ask Wesley about it in private. She quickly heeded his command and left the conference room to retrieve the phone messages from his office.

The entire room remained awkwardly still as Wesley fumbled to get his papers in order. They were all quite curious about what was happening to him as well, but instead of asking, the staff feigned light conversations with one another so as to not draw attention to their well-respected leader.

See, most of the crew had been with Wesley since he opened the firm thirteen years ago. Back then, Wesley had just dropped out of Emory Law School after only one year, deciding instead to pursue a career in the one thing *he knew* he was good at: spinning. So he hired Atlanta's top head-hunting agency and robbed the second best person from each of the public relations departments of Atlanta's most powerful companies: CNN, UPS, Coca-Cola, Delta Airlines and The Home Depot. His only directive to the headhunter? *Double their salaries.* And just like that, Wesley built a loyal, racially diverse and formidable public relations team who considered themselves the *X-Men* of their industry.

Lilly finally returned with a stack of pink lined papers and handed them to Wesley. He quickly shuffled through the messages until he landed on the one with *Ava DeSantis* scribbled across the top. He removed it from the stack, angrily shred it to pieces, and then shoved the pieces of pink paper one by one into an abandoned Coke can nearby.

Everyone in the room took note of his odd behavior.

"Okay, folks. Where are we?"

Ed cautiously raised his hand. "I've got *The Journal* rerunning the Emerald Club expose from three years ago. My source tells me that Miss Vinson stirred up interest in that story again."

"Good. What else?"

The timid Indian woman raised her hand.

"Yes, Amoli. Go ahead."

"I ran a full background check on Saffroy's wife and teenaged children. They're clean."

"Good. What about Saffroy himself?"

"Not so good. If titty bars gave out frequent flyer miles, this chump would be in Tahiti."

The room burst out laughing; hearing a comment like that come out of such a shy woman cracked up even the most humorless members of the group.

The sexy receptionist entered the room, slicing through the laughter. She waltzed her tall red heels to the very end of the table, handing Wesley a steaming hot white coffee mug.

"Here you go, sir."

"Hold our calls."

"Of course. Anything else?" Lola's sparkling amber eyes behind her glasses reminded Wesley that she's there for the taking.

"No, not at this time. Thank you." Given his weakened state, Wesley could not keep from looking at her large breasts dangling in front of him. "I'm sorry, Amoli. Please continue."

The Indian woman drew a deep breath and continued in her sweet accent. "It appears that Mister Saffroy has a real penchant for blondes. He goes to strip bars at least once a week and spends shit loads of money on the dancers. At least that's what Rick Houston, the manager of the Rocking Horse, told me last night."

"So it's possible Saffroy knew Vinson when she worked at the Emerald Club?"

"Yes, sir, it's a real possibility."

"Perhaps that's how Sarah Vinson got her job?" added Dierdra.

Ed jumped in. "Now we have motive."

"Right, 'you owe me bitch, give it up,'" added Loretta, the middle-aged black woman.

Wesley looked at Amoli. "Did you find out the last time Saffroy was at the Rocking Horse?"

"Yes. He was there last night. I saw him myself."

The room gasped.

"Are you sure it was him?" asked Lilly.

"Yes. I ran his background check that afternoon so I know what he looks like. I watched him pay for two lap dances while I was there."

"Shit!" Wesley was angry. "Lilly, call Daniel Holt right now. Tell him to tell Saffroy to *stay the fuck home*. He is not to go anywhere but work and home!"

"Got it." Lilly rocketed from her seat and exited.

"What else?"

"That's all I have sir."

"Good work, Amoli...Who else?"

Awkward silence filled the room.

"Come on, people. What else do we have?"

Derek chimed in. "That's all, sir. We've hit a brick wall."

"You hit a brick wall? What the fuck is that?"

Derek was too ashamed to reply.

"Y'all are public relations *professionals*. There's no such thing as a fucking brick wall! Your job is to go out and find every single piece of goddamn information that's out there about every single—"

The receptionist interrupted. "Excuse me, Mr. Scarborough. Ava DeSantis is on line two."

"I said hold *all* of our calls, Lola." Wesley was visibly annoyed.

"But she said it was an emergency."

Wesley completely lost his temper. "I said take a fucking message!"

The whole room was frozen. Wesley had never yelled that loudly before.

"Yes, of course." Lola hung her blonde-ponytailed head low and left the room.

A sonic wave of silence filled the room.

Ed ventured to break the ice. "Maybe I can fly to Louisville in the morning and see what I can find out from her high school buddies?"

"Good idea," added Lilly.

"I can go back to the Rocking Horse tonight and do damage control," said Amoli.

"I'll go with her," added Dierdra. "We'll make sure no one remembers seeing Saffroy. We'll just need to take enough petty cash to make them forget."

Wesley glared at all of them. He couldn't believe Ava DeSantis had the nerve to call him at work again.

Lola timidly returned. "I'm sorry to interrupt again, Mr. Scarborough, but your wife is on line four. I think it's the baby?"

"Everyone. Go."

The ScarCom Gang scurried out.

Wesley took the call on a multi-line phone in the corner of the conference room.

"I'm on my way home now, honey."

"Hello, Wesley."

Wesley was shocked. "Ava?"

"For some strange reason, I feel like you're trying to avoid me."

Wesley's blood boiled through his tanned skin. "Didn't my mother finish paying you?"

"Yes. Earlier this year, why?"

"Then this conversation is over." Wesley slammed the phone down and stormed out of the conference room.

Lola sat quietly reading an issue of *Vogue* magazine when Wesley marched upon her desk. "If you ever put that woman's call through again, you better dust off your fucking resume and buy a book of stamps. Are we clear?"

Lilly stood nearby with Ed, watching the verbal attack.

"But Mr. Scarborough—"

"No more fucking excuses, Lola. You need to filter my calls or find another job!"

"But your wife is still holding for you on line four."

Wesley was astonished. Lola picked up the phone receiver and handed it to him on the spot.

"Michelle?"

"Hey, what took you so long?"

"I'm sorry. I just got tied up—"

"I feel awful about last night. I want you to come home."

"Is the baby all right?"

"Well, yes, I'm still pregnant if that's what you're asking. Just come home. I feel awful. I'll make a picnic lunch for us. I could even meet you at Piedmont Park?"

"I wish I could, Michelle, but I can't leave now. There's way too much going on."

"What about tonight then? I can make a romantic dinner. Anything you want."

"Tonight? Okay, tonight will work."

Lilly overheard Wesley's conversation. "You have dinner tonight with your parents."

"Shit. I forgot we have dinner with my parents tonight."

"Oh."

"Don't worry, honey. I'm not upset with you. I'll be home no later than five, okay?"

"Okay, baby. I'll see you then."

Wesley humbly hung up the phone. Lola, now afraid to make eye contact with him, excused herself and headed to the restroom.

Lilly moved in closer to Wesley. "I don't know what your problem is, but whatever it is, you better leave it where you found it because it's bringing us all down, Wes."

"I'm sorry, I've got a lot on my mind."

"I know, Wes, we all do."

"No, Lilly," Wesley's sharp blue eyes peered into her soul, "you have no *fucking* idea what I'm going through."

CHAPTER 20

A Tale Of Two Wesleys

TUESDAY, OCTOBER 10, 2006
11:15 A.M.

Michelle was lying face down on her fluffy white living room sofa, trying to give her back a break from the weight of her belly while watching *Dr. Phil* on television. She was still in her plaid flannel pajamas from the night before, but her hair was already styled, and her thick *Betty Boop* eyelashes were all ready to go…ready for dinner with the in-laws five long hours from now.

Instead of focusing on Dr. Phil's inspiring story of a homeless woman's venture into the competitive world of cupcake bake-offs, Michelle was busy running embarrassing labor scenarios in her mind. *What if I defecate in front of everyone? Won't it smell up the room?* Dr. Phil's eyes widened as he tasted the homeless cook's legendary cupcake. *Wait, what if they need to give me an episiotomy and then I crap myself? Oh my God, I'll never be tight again.*

The doorbell RANG, interrupting Michelle's troubled thoughts.

Please Lord, not Miriam. I can't do twice in one day.
Michelle struggled to climb up the white sofa and waddled
to the foyer mirror to check her make-up. *Fat, but pretty.*
Fat, but pretty. Michelle had been saying this to herself
multiple times a day, hoping it would inspire her to take off
the forty pounds of baby weight she'd gained over the last
nine months. On a small frame like hers, forty pounds rep-
resented more than thirty percent of her body weight –
a real disaster if her former beauty pageant coaches ever
found out.

The doorbell RANG again. Michelle finally mustered
the courage to grab the brass door handle and open it.

Outside, it was a perfect sunny, cool day. And there,
standing on the stone-floored doorstep, was a gorgeous,
tall woman with long, straight platinum blonde hair.
She was holding a three-foot, dark cellophane-wrapped
gift basket in her arms with a wine bottle and imported
food items packed neatly within. Her dark oval sunglasses covered most of her elegant face, leaving only a perfect porcelain nose and shiny red lips beneath them. In
fact, she looked as if she had just stepped out of a Tom
Ford ad, wearing a low-cut black jumpsuit with a yellow
Hobo shoulder bag and matching yellow spike heels...Yes,

Studio 54 disco attire at eleven o'clock in the morning. Perfectly normal for Buckhead.

"Welcome to the neighborhood!" she said in a deep, barely Southern accent.

"Oh, how precious!"

The woman moved the gift basket away from her face and handed it to Michelle.

"Thank you so much for this. I'm Michelle Scarborough."

"Pleasure to meet you, Michelle. My name is Ava. Ava DeSantis."

<hr />

Ava sat on a stool at the black granite breakfast bar, elegantly sipping a tall, cut crystal glass of iced tea while Michelle straightened up the kitchen.

"I agree, I just love that store. Which is really sad because I haven't been there in forever," shared Michelle. "Well, you know, they never carry anything over a size six, and right now I would *die* to get into a size six."

"Well, since I'm tall I usually have to stick with designer clothes."

"How tall *are* you if you don't mind me asking?"

"Five-foot-ten last time I was barefoot," said Ava wryly. "Which had to be years ago."

Michelle rolled her eyes, mouth open. "Uggh. I would just die to look like you. You look like a fashion model."

"That's very sweet."

"Hard to believe you're just a housewife like me."

Ava smiled uncomfortably. "Well, that I am."

"So, which house is yours again?"

"The two-story colonial on the corner."

"Oh, the one with the huge magnolia tree right in the front yard?"

"Yes, that's it."

"Aww, I love that house. How big is it?"

Ava looked up to the sky, conjuring a credible answer. "Five-and-a-half-thousand feet I believe?"

"Really. This one is only four thousand. I told Wesley we should start small, but I'm already regretting my decision."

"No, you have a beautiful home. It's perfect. Too much to clean if you go any larger. Well, too much for someone else to clean."

"Exactly. I mean, we use to live in my husband's *huge* home in Ansley Park before we moved here. It was totally gorgeous and built in 1800 or something, but I could not get a decent night's sleep there to save my life. I think it was haunted."

Ava visibly reacted.

"Do you believe in ghosts, Ava?"

Ava leaned in, shooting her hypnotic gaze across the kitchen. "Only when they come back for a good reason."

Michelle smiled back. "I hear ya." She then walked over to the Sub-Zero refrigerator. "Can I get you more tea?"

"No, thank you. This is fine. I need to run soon anyway."

"Oh, no, please stay. I don't get many visitors here. In fact, you're the first one actually, besides my mother-in-law, who's a real meanie. Jesus, I can't stand her."

Ava's eyes darkened. "We can't win them all."

"How about you. Do you get along with your mother-in-law?"

"Yes, she's deceased. Best type of mother-in-law to have."

Michelle chuckled. "So what does your husband do for a living?"

"He's a pilot with Delta. In fact, he's pulling into Tokyo right now as we speak."

"Nice. Do you have any kids?"

Ava smiled wide. "Well, actually, Wesley and I are expecting our first child in May."

"No! You're kidding?"

"Why? Don't I look like the mothering type?"

"No, I mean, yes, of course you do. Did you say your husband's name is Wesley?"

"Yes, it is."

"Holy cow. My husband's name is Wesley too! Isn't that wild?"

"Yes. What a strange coincidence."

"Not like it's a really common name or anything. I can't wait to tell my Wesley when he gets home tonight."

Ava sipped her tea, trying to suppress a smile.

"So how far along are you? You aren't showing at all."

"Almost eleven weeks. I'm in the twenty-four hour morning sickness stage right now. I can barely keep anything solid down."

Michelle waddled to the pantry and pulled out a skinny box of saltine crackers. "Take these. They practically saved my life."

"Oh, thank you." Ava took the box of crackers from Michelle's hand, and placed them on the breakfast bar.

"But try not to eat too many or you'll wind up looking like a hippo like me." Michelle cracked a self-deprecating smile when the cordless phone on the countertop RANG. Michelle moved to answer it. "Excuse me."

"Of course." Ava got up from her stool and headed toward the adjacent white living room as Michelle spoke on the phone.

"Hello?...Oh, hey, Miss Eloise..."

Ava shrewdly turned her attention to the phone conversation in the kitchen.

"...Yes, ma'am. We'll definitely be there by six...Do you need us to pick up anything on the way in?...Are you sure?...Okay, we'll see y'all tonight...Yes, six o'clock sharp."

Michelle hung up the phone. "Damn, you'd think we were having dinner at the White House."

"Well their home *does* look like the White House."

Michelle was taken aback. "How did you know that?" Michelle was now standing behind Ava in the living room.

Ava turned and cracked a quarter smile. "I assumed your in-laws live here," she pointed to an 8x10 photo of

Michelle and Wesley in wedding attire, standing in front of a mansion that looked like a replica of the White House. The framed picture was part of a dozen family photos grouped together on a baby grand piano in the corner of the room.

"Yes, that is their home. Good eye," said Michelle, strangely relieved. "It's called Scarborough Mansion, as in the Scarborough furniture family. We were married there."

"Old money. Charming."

Ava continued looking at the other framed photos on the piano...like the one of Wesley beaming in his college graduation gown...and the one of Wesley celebrating his first year at ScarCom...and the one of Michelle being hoisted in the air by ten cheerleader bridesmaids...and the most recent photo of Wesley and Michelle at the beach; a heart-tugging scene of Wesley tenderly kissing Michelle's swollen belly as she smiles down upon him wearing a turquoise bikini.

Ava's stomach churned as her eyes zoomed in on Wesley kissing his unborn baby. "You have a very handsome husband."

"Thank you."

"Very blonde, like me." Ava finally turned away from the photo. "Your son will be beautiful."

"Yes, thank you. I can't wait to meet him." Michelle lovingly rubbed her tummy.

Vomit began rising up Ava's throat, making her turn away from the scene.

"Are you okay?" asked Michelle.

"Yes, yes, I'm fine."

"Do you need crackers?"

"No, it'll pass. And your Wesley? What does he do for a living?"

Michelle was concerned for Ava, but continued the conversation. "He owns a PR firm downtown. It specializes in helping law firms publicize big cases or something like that. And he literally works day and night for his stupid clients…At least that's what he tells me."

Bingo. Ava finally straightened up and rejoined the conversation. "Really."

"Sure, I mean, you know how it is being married to a successful man. We had problems early on with him flirting and all, but we worked it out."

"I'm sure he's one hundred percent faithful given your sweet disposition."

"Well, I hope so. And I think he is…But sometimes you have to wonder about a good-looking man who stays overnight in his office all the time, right? I mean, don't you worry about your husband? Flying around the world with all those pretty flight attendants?"

"No, not really." Ava gave her a look of unbreakable confidence.

"Well, you should see how many women *throw* themselves at my husband, sometimes right in front of me! And if they find out he's a Scarborough, forget it. Makes me sick just thinking about it."

"And how *did* you two meet?"

"Believe it or not, I was just a travel nurse before I got married. Wesley was over at his best friend's home for dinner while I was there treating their son for the flu. Little Sebastian junior."

Ava suddenly became dizzy.

"Soooo sad, his best friend just died last week. Thirty-six years old from a heart attack. Can you believe it? Wesley is still so devastated."

Ava became off balance. "I'm sorry, where's your bathroom?"

"It's right there. Let me help you."

Ava tried to walk, but almost fell. Michelle quickly assisted Ava – still stumbling in her yellow heels – over to the cornflower blue powder room near the front door. After a few seconds, Ava broke free from Michelle, rushed into the bathroom and slammed the door.

Michelle stood outside the door listening to the sounds of Ava throwing up violently. "I'm so glad we can bond like this," said Michelle jokingly. "I'll get you a case of saltines next time I go to the store."

<hr />

Ava rinsed her mouth with water as she stared at herself in the mirror. Her large woodsy-green eyes were filling with revenge. *How dare you flaunt your unborn baby in my face.* Her eyes darkened in the mirror. *And to watch that fat demon make three kids after what he did to me? What kind of man are you? Tell me? Who the fuck are you? You fucking son of a whoring bitch!*

"Are you okay in there?" asked Michelle outside the door.

"Just washing up," replied Ava in a sing-songy manner. She then rinsed her mouth one last time and shut off the water. As she reached for the decorative hand towel, she noticed a bottle of nail polish and an old-fashioned, sharp metal nail file on the marble countertop.

Ava picked up the knife-like nail file, examining it closely. She held it tighter and tighter and tighter in her grasp.

"Just let me know if you need anything," said the innocent lamb on the other side of the door.

Ava gripped the nail file with all her might as she slowly reached for the doorknob.

"Trust me, it gets better in a few weeks," shouted Michelle.

Ava's large green eyes were turning black with murderous rage...

"You really are sick in there, aren't you?"

Silence.

"Ava...Are you okay?"

Silence.

Then suddenly Ava SPRUNG OPEN the door, leapt out of the bathroom and shoved the metal file into Michelle's face. In response, Michelle bent backwards, *terrified*.

"I can't believe they still make these." Ava stood cool and calm as a Druid tree.

Michelle breathed heavily for a few moments...then started laughing, recovering from the false alarm.

"Oh, did I scare you? Bless your heart."

Michelle continued laughing at herself. "You scared the hell out of me. *How silly?*"

Ava joined in on the laughter. "How rude of me. I am so sorry"

"And yes, they do still make those. I'll grab you one next time I go to Piggly Wiggly."

<hr />

Ava stood outside on the doorstep as Michelle remained inside, saying good-bye.

"Again, I am so sorry I scared you like that. I should be more careful opening doors that quickly," shared Ava.

"Oh, please don't worry, it's my fault. I'm a total mess without my Prozac."

"Listen, if you need absolutely anything while your husband's at work, just give me a call. I'm always out running errands, so just call my cell before you swing by." Ava dug into her yellow shoulder bag, searching for a pen and paper to write down her number. While doing this,

Michelle noticed a pack of Marlborough Red cigarettes in her bag.

"Are you still smoking?" asked Michelle.

Ava thought quickly. "Heavens, no. I don't smoke. I just keep these in my purse in case my Wesley goes into a nicotine fit."

Michelle smiled back in relief. "Well, thanks again for the gift basket. It's so pretty, I hate to open it."

"Oh, but you must. There's tons of delicious goodies in there. And you might as well eat them now before you start your diet." Ava's eyes sparkled behind her oval sunglasses.

"It was great meeting you, Ava," Michelle stepped out to give her a hug. In return, Ava felt an unusual twitch of friendly affection.

"Pleasure meeting you as well." Ava strutted down the circular driveway in her kick-ass yellow heels. "Good luck with the baby if I don't see you before the big day!"

"Thanks, you too!"

Ava watched over her shoulder as Michelle closed and locked the door. Seconds later, she diverted her direction, walking over to the opposite side of the street.

Around the corner, Ava dug into her bag, grabbed a cigarette and lit it as she walked towards a canary yellow Lamborghini Gallardo parked behind a community garbage dumpster.

Ava opened the car door, shoved the key in and REVVED up the engine…

Welcome to the neighborhood, Wesley.

CHAPTER 21

THE GIFT BASKET

TUESDAY, OCTOBER 10, 2006
5:32 P.M.

Michelle sat at an ivory, antique make-up boudoir in her master bedroom, wearing a bright purple fuzzy robe. She scrutinized the pores on her face in the mirror as she re-curled each section of her dark, thick hair with a curling iron. *Fat, but pretty. Fat, but pretty.*

Wesley stood nearby, naked and freshly showered, trying to find a suitable pair of underwear in the large cherry wood dresser. "We're not late. Besides, they can learn how to wait for people."

"But Miss Eloise called to remind us to be on time."

"That's not my problem." Wesley pulled out a pair of orange tight-fitting briefs and stepped into them.

"Wes, I hate making your mother mad. She's unbearable if she doesn't get her way."

"I don't want to talk about this anymore." Wesley headed into the bathroom to finish getting ready. He opened the medicine cabinet and pulled out a can of shaving cream.

"Hey, who gave us that gift basket in the living room?"

Michelle continued fussing with her hair. "Oh, that's from our new neighbor. She lives in the two-story house on the corner of Maplewood and Pine."

Wesley slathered shaving cream across his tanned, chiseled chin.

"It's so pretty I don't even want to open it up. Plus, I'm sure it's just the usual stuff. Stale cheese and raspberry tarts that everyone sticks in those. I'm just touched she came over to meet me. Very nice gesture."

Wesley opened the drawer and took out his large, single-bladed razor. "Yes, very nice."

"Oh, I forgot to tell you!"

Wesley turned on the faucet. The water was LOUD.

"Her name is Ava and, of all things, her husband's name is Wesley too! Isn't that funny?"

Wesley turned off the water. "What? I can't hear you."

"I said her husband's name is Wesley too. Isn't that funny?"

"Yes, very funny." Uninterested in the conversation, Wesley turned the water back on and starting shaving.

"He's an airline pilot for Delta, and she stays at home bored to death like me. Oh, and she's pregnant with their first child too. I think they're gonna be great neighbors."

"That's nice." Wesley flinched from cutting a small slit under his nose.

Then, suddenly it dawned upon him. He shut the water off and hurried back into the bedroom...

"What's wrong, Wes?"

His face said it all. "Did you remember to swing by the dry cleaners today?"

CHAPTER 22

DINNER AT THE WHITE HOUSE

TUESDAY, OCTOBER 10, 2006
6:18 P.M.

Wesley drove his black Cadillac Escalade up to the front entrance of *Scarborough Mansion* – a spectacular, twenty-five thousand-square-foot home designed to be one-half the size of its big brother on 1600 Pennsylvania Avenue. Wesley looked over to Michelle's belly with affectionate eyes. "Someday, you will be the king of this castle," he said.

Michelle beamed in the passenger seat. "And so will you."

Miss Eloise, dressed in her traditional black and white maid uniform, greeted Wesley and Michelle in the grandiose white and gray marbled foyer. Her round, dark face contorted into an expression of pure joy. "You look adorable, honey! Like Snow White ate a dwarf!" She gave Michelle a big, warm hug. "How ya feelin'?"

Michelle chuckled in her light pink cocktail dress. "I feel great, Miss Eloise. Thank you."

"And you, Wesley! You sure did a fine job with those newspaper people yesterday. We all watched you on TV, and we was *glued!*" Miss Eloise kissed Wesley on the cheek. His blonde slicked back hair, red satin shirt and black dress pants looked stunning against the white and gray marbled entrance of the home. "Even your daddy was proud of you," she whispered into his ear.

"Speaking of the Devil, where is he?" asked Wesley.

Miriam walked up to the foyer wearing a crimson Chanel suit, nude high heels and a classic blonde Ivana Trump up-do. "You know I don't like that word used in my home, Wesley." Miriam of course, looked magnificent for her age. As with all other blood-sucking creatures, evil kept her from ever aging a day over forty. She stiffly kissed Wesley on the cheek. "Your father's still getting ready." She then looked at Michelle, and gave her a cardboard hug. "Hello, sugar. Looks like you swallowed a basketball down there."

Michelle attempted to smile.

Moments later, sixty-five-year-old Thomas Scarborough – as in the Honorable United States District Court Judge Thomas J. Scarborough – made his grand entrance down the *Gone with the Wind* inspired double staircase. He was a tall, extraordinarily handsome older man, with dark brown eyes and a full head of sharply contrasting salt and pepper hair, with a well-trimmed beard and mustache to match. He wore a casual tuxedo (as he always did for private dinners) and looked like the kind of man that could have won the 1876 presidency based on his looks and wealth alone. But what truly made Thomas Scarborough special was his larger than life charismatic personality, a black hole celebrity that instantly stole the light from anyone close by.

"Well, good evening, everybody! I am *so honored* that y'all were able to finally fit us into your busy schedules and grace us with your tremendous charm, original wit and hereditary good looks!"

Wesley rolled his eyes. "Ahhh. Let the guilt tripping begin."

Thomas finished walking down the staircase and approached Wesley. "Well, son, it's only a guilt trip if you have something to feel guilty about." He reached out and gave Wesley a huge bear hug, then jokingly tossed Wesley aside, grabbed Michelle, kissed her on both cheeks, then bent over wildly smooching her belly.

Michelle giggled uncontrollably.

Afterwards, Thomas stood up and announced: "Now that all of the bullshit pleasantries are out of the way, how about we enjoy a few cocktails? Eloise, bust out the whiskey!"

All four were seated at the north end of a sixteen-person, carved mahogany dining room table fit for a royal estate. Miss Eloise was in the background, preparing to serve the meal.

"I know, wasn't he fabulous?" shared Michelle. "I tell him all the time that was born to be a TV talk show host."

Wesley smiled humbly. "Thanks, baby."

"Everyone's talking about the case, Wesley, especially at church. Last night, we spent an entire hour exploring why some women are willing to subject themselves to public humiliation all in the name of money," said Miriam. "It's a new form of gold-digging."

"I'm not so sure the girl is lying," added Thomas.

Miriam puffed out her large, manufactured chest. "How can you say that, Thomas? Haven't you been reading the papers? The girl was a prostitute before she became a paralegal. I think that's enough cause for reasonable doubt."

Wesley shot Michelle a look that said: *here we go again.*

"Well, whatever really happened will eventually come out."

Miriam smiled softly. "Lies can stay buried for years, Thomas. You know that."

Thomas sharpened his gaze. "The Honorable Walter F. George once said that the truth *always* comes to light in order to demolish those who stand in its way… And I, with all of my heart, believe this statement to be true."

Wesley was internally troubled by his words.

"As you can see, your father is very fond of defense attorneys," joked Miriam.

"Well, I *married* you, didn't I?" he replied.

Michelle naively jumped into the crossfire. "You know, I still can't figure out how you two ever hooked up, let alone stayed married for thirty-seven years?"

Thomas and Miriam exchanged a look.

"Opposites attract," said Miriam.

"Either that, or I'm a masochist at heart!" laughed Thomas.

Michelle giggled again, as she always did after Thomas spoke. She genuinely loved him more than her own father: a thrice-divorced, drunken truck mechanic in Tifton, Georgia.

"So how many days do we have before my beautiful baby arrives?" asked Thomas.

"Technically three, but my doctor said that only ten percent of babies are actually born on their due date."

"Wesley was born on his due date, practically on the hour," said Miriam.

"Never met a Scarborough man who didn't show up on time," added Thomas.

Wesley looked at Michelle's large pink belly. "No pressure, little guy. No pressure."

Michelle crouched her eyebrows with sarcasm. "Yeah, right."

"So, have we decided on a name yet?" asked Thomas.

"They said they wouldn't announce the name until after the baby arrived," interjected Miriam. "As I recall, Michelle's family has some sort of...superstition about such things."

"Well, actually, we have a surprise for you both tonight."

Miriam and Thomas perked up.

"A name?" asked Miriam.

Michelle smiled. "Yes."

"Well, what is it?" begged Thomas.

Wesley cleared his throat for dramatic effect. "We're naming the baby…Thomas James Scarborough." Thomas and Miriam erupted into pure joy.

"We'll call him T.J. for short," added Michelle. "It was my idea."

"That's wonderful!" added Miss Eloise. "Baby T.J."

Thomas leaned over to Wesley. "Now *that's* what I wanted to name you, but of course your mother had other plans."

"I can't wait to tell Aunt Mary," said Miriam.

Thomas pointed to Michelle's belly. "Now I'll save my monogramed dress shirts for the little one since we've got the same name." He then stood up and raised his champagne glass full of whiskey. "A toast…to the arrival of the future heir of the Scarborough dynasty. May he be as smart as his grammy, as gorgeous as his momma, and have much better taste in furniture than his pappy!"

Everyone laughed and toasted. "Here, here."

Miss Eloise served the first course of the meal: a bowl of white, creamy lobster bisque. Michelle licked her lips.

"I'm so hungry, I could eat a horse and chase down the jockey!"

Miriam reacted. "So have you thought about a plan yet to lose the baby weight?"

Miss Eloise, still serving the soup, exchanged a look with Thomas.

"No, not yet. I'm just worried about getting through labor first."

"Well, I lost all of my baby weight with Wesley the day after he was born."

Thomas reacted.

"But then again I only gained about twelve pounds during my pregnancy. How much have you gained? Forty-five? Fifty?"

"At my last appointment, twenty-five pounds."

Wesley was proud of Michelle for fibbing.

"Twenty-five? I doubt that, sugar. I can see a difference every time we meet."

"Miriam," said Thomas abruptly. "Eat your soup before it gets cold, darlin'."

Miriam ignored him. "Well, start thinking about it now because it's very important that you start watching your figure again. You used to be a very attractive girl."

Michelle reacted shamefully. Wesley slowly angered.

"A man like my son needs to have a beautiful, svelte wife by his side at all times. It's very important for his public image."

Thomas dropped his spoon on the table. "Darlin', why don't we go into the kitchen and help Miss Eloise serve the next course."

"I prefer to stay here, Thomas."

"Come on, sweet cakes. Keep me company."

Wesley shot Thomas a look that said, *thank you.*

"I'm not that hungry anyway." Miriam begrudgingly threw her napkin on the table and exited the dining room. Thomas quickly followed.

Wesley whispered to Michelle. "I'm sorry, baby. You deserve better than this."

Michelle became emotional. "No, she's right. Your mother is always right."

Thomas and Miriam entered the kitchen. It was a gigantic, stainless steel commercial kitchen with equipment usually reserved for high-end restaurants. Miss Eloise stood by the triple-decker oven, waiting for her baked chicken to crisp before serving.

"I know what you're going to say," said Miriam.

"I'll save my breath then," replied Thomas.

"I am *so tired* of you always trying to control what I do, what I say and how I say it. I can't wait until that baby finally gets here!"

"I'm counting down the days like Christmas myself."

Eloise smirked as she opened the top stove and checked on the chicken.

"Can't you see that Michelle has become an embarrassment to our family, Thomas? You and I both know Wesley can do better than her. She just needs to be reminded of that before she gets fat and makes a mockery of my son."

"You mean *our* son."

"He's only yours by name, Thomas. And even *that* may be in question. Your dead sperm probably wasn't even good enough to make him."

Thomas was unmoved by Miriam's emotional spear, for this was not the first time she hinted that Wesley may not be his biological son. And in the back of his mind, he knew that this was indeed a possibility...The evidence? Miriam's three-month affair with a twenty-year-old Swedish tennis instructor around the same time Wesley was conceived. Couple this with Thomas' inability to father any other children since Wesley's birth in 1970. But for the sake of all things, neither Miriam nor Thomas ever formally requested a DNA test. No, Heaven forbid. And for obvious reasons, they both made sure Wesley never suspected a thing.

"Miriam, with all of the murderers, rapists and child molesters that have stepped into my courtroom over the years, I can honestly say that you are the coldest bitch I have ever laid eyes upon."

Miriam slapped Thomas *hard* across the face.

"As soon as that baby arrives, I am going to file. That means you only have a few days left to live in this house. I hope you've got *your slaves* starting to pack for you now."

Miriam shot Eloise a dirty look then exited the kitchen. After she left, Eloise and Thomas stood together, side by side near the stove in silence.

"Remind me to not throw a party the day that woman dies," said Eloise. "I wouldn't want to see Jesus dancing in a conga line."

Thomas gave Eloise a serious look, then ruptured with laughter. "Well, hell. *I* sure would!" He mimicked dancing with an invisible conga line, right there in the kitchen.

"Don't mind her, sir. You'll be a free man soon enough."

Thomas continued conga dancing by himself. "That's right, I'll be a free man. A free man? A free man!" Thomas pulled Eloise from the stove and conga danced her around the kitchen. "Yeah, baby, a free man! Whoo hoo!"

Eloise laughed hysterically. "You so crazy."

Thomas stopped the dance, turned her around and gave her a loud kiss on the cheek. "But I'm sure as hell gonna miss you, Eloise!"

"Please. You know I'm gonna come visit."

Later that evening, all four had returned to the dining room table, silently eating cheesecake and sipping coffee.

The phone RANG loudly nearby. Miss Eloise answered it in the adjacent serving suite. "Scarborough residence...Yes, ma'am, this is, how can I help you?...No, I haven't seen him this evening..." Miss Eloise shot Wesley a look of concern. "...May I ask who's calling?"

Wesley's heart started beating like a bass drum. *Fuck.*

"No, I'm sorry he's not. You may want to try him at another number...Yes, ma'am, you too. Have a good night." Eloise hung up the phone and shot Wesley another look.

Wesley was worried. Seconds later, his cell phone RANG.

The table noticed.

"I hate those things, Wesley. Could you please turn it off at the table?" asked Miriam.

"Yes, I'll turn it off."

"Wait. What if it's Lilly?" asked Michelle.

The phone continued RINGING. Wesley quietly looked at the caller ID:

Unknown Caller

He debated letting the call go to voicemail, but since his staff often used disposable pre-paid cell phones during investigations, he answered it abruptly. "I'm having dinner right now. This better be good."

"Meet me at the club on Fourteenth and Belvedere," said Ava on the other line in her deep voice laced with a mild New Jersey accent.

"How did you get this number?"

"Be there. Ten o'clock."

"I'm sorry, I can't tonight."

The table now peered at Wesley for talking on the phone.

"I hope your wife liked the gift basket I brought her today."

Wesley's stomach sank to the floor. His pool blue eyes widened with fear.

"Just wear something nice."

CLICK. Ava hung up the line.

"Tonight? Wow. That's late, Lilly, but I'll be there," said Wesley to the dial tone on the other side. "All right, see you then." He quickly pressed END CALL and placed the phone down on the table.

"What was that all about?" asked Miriam.

"This Saffroy case. It's eating us alive. I need to get back to the office tonight."

Michelle, sitting closest to Wesley, was devastated. She missed the first part of the conversation but overheard the loud dial tone while Wesley pretended to speak with Lilly. "Excuse me," she said quietly as she rose from the table and headed to the bathroom nearby.

Wesley and Miriam continued eating their cheesecake in silence, while Thomas glared at Wesley.

"So, Lilly calls your cell phone regularly?" asked Miriam.

"Yes, she calls me day and night."

"Then why did you ask her how she found your number?" continued Miriam.

Thomas looked at his son with severe disappointment.

"I was being sarcastic, mother. Why are you always so damn critical?"

"Because I raised you better than that," she replied.

"Yes, Miriam. You raised him to be just like you, a professional liar," added Thomas. He moved his napkin from his lap and rose from the table. "Your wife is about to give birth any minute, boy. How could you be so stupid?"

"What? I don't understand?" replied Wesley.

The air thickened in the room. Time appeared to stand still. "Son, you have no idea how much I would give up for a chance to start over with you." He then walked away from the table and exited the dining room.

Wesley cradled his head in his hands. "Shit."

Miriam continued picking at her dessert, shaking her head like a disappointed schoolmarm.

Everyone but Thomas stood in the foyer saying good-bye.

"Now, which way do I turn when I go through the hospital main entrance?" asked Miriam.

"I can email you the instructions they gave me if you like," replied Michelle.

While they were speaking, Miss Eloise pulled Wesley aside. "Before you leave, let me show you what I've done with your old tennis trophies in the library right quick." She shot him a look that said, *come with me*. Automatically, Wesley followed.

When they arrived in the library, Eloise stopped and whispered: "You better do something about that crazy girl from college before your father finds out."

Wesley was stunned. "You know about her?"

"Of course I know about her, Wesley. There ain't nothin' that goes on in this family that I don't know about."

"Yes, ma'am, I know that."

"And you know that I been in this house raising your daddy since he was ten years old, and that I love him just as much as I love my own nephews."

"Yes, I do."

"And you know that it would tear his heart to pieces if he knew anything about you and that girl, and what we did after."

"He'd never speak to me again."

"You damn straight. Now out of nowhere, that girl is calling your momma, at least once a day, sometimes twice. And she's *refusing* to talk to her. Pretty soon, your daddy is gonna start asking questions."

"Shit."

"You need to handle this, Wesley."

"What should I do?"

"Find out what the hell she wants and give it to her so she'll leave this family alone."

"I'll do my best."

"Good. Now, go home and be a good husband to that beautiful bride of yours, and forget we even talked about this, you hear?"

"Yes, ma'am."

Miss Eloise gave Wesley a warm hug, beaming her wide gap-tooth smile to the sky...

As Wesley stared into the book-lined abyss, unsure of what to do next.

Wesley and Michelle did not speak for most of the drive home. There was no traffic, not even another car on the road. It was bizarrely empty for a usually busy weeknight in Buckhead. But tonight, it was so dark and silent that it felt as if the world had ended and just the two of them – still arguing – had survived.

"Are you mad at me?" asked Michelle.

"No. I just don't want you talking to our neighbors."

"Why?"

"It's too risky."

"But I don't—"

"Like that woman who brought you the gift basket today? She's trouble, Michelle. Stay away from her."

"You mean Ava?"

Wesley was shocked. "She told you her name? Why didn't you tell me?"

"I *did* tell you her name but you never listen to me! Remember I told you that her husband's name is Wesley too? Ava and Wesley. I told you!"

"Don't say those names together."

Michelle was confused. "What the hell is wrong with you?"

"I just don't want you talking to those people. Period."

Silence.

Michelle started to cry…"I'm sorry I've embarrassed you by getting fat."

"What? Michelle, that's not what I mean…"

"I've always known that I'm not good enough for you, but now I just don't know what to do about it," Michele whined through her tears.

"Stop that. You know not to listen to my mother! She just says stupid things. She doesn't mean anything by it."

Michelle turned her head away to look out the black window.

"You're a beautiful woman, Michelle. And I am very proud to call you my wife."

"Then why don't you want me talking to the neighbors?"

"Because Ava is *not* our neighbor," he thought on his feet. "She's a reporter trying to take advantage of *you* to get information about *me*."

"That's crazy."

"Well it's true...I saw her at the press conference on Monday."

"And how do you even *know* what she looks like?"

Wesley was caught. "I mean, I know her name. I know who she is. She's a reporter for some political website."

"Well, we can settle this right now." Michelle unlocked her seatbelt, grabbed her pink Prada purse from the floor and began digging through it.

"What are you doing?"

"She gave me her cell phone number. I'll call her right now so we can settle this once and for all…"

"*No!*" Wesley yelled at the top of his lungs. "Don't do that!"

Michelle was stunned, literally frozen in place with her pink Prada purse held tightly in her grasp. Wesley had never yelled at her before. And to yell at her while she was in such a fragile condition was beyond comprehension.

Her innocent face crumbled like a baby about to cry.

"I'm sorry, Michelle, I don't know. Maybe *I am* just being paranoid."

Michelle was too heartbroken to respond.

"You're right, I think I may have her mixed up with someone else. I'm just under so much pressure right now, I don't even know half of what's coming out of my mouth...I'm sorry, baby. I won't bother you about this anymore." He looked at the clock on the dashboard. It was nine thirty.

"You're getting paranoid, Wes, and it's making me crazy," she said like a disappointed child. "Please take some time off from this case. I need you to be strong for me in the delivery room...I'm scared."

Wesley turned onto their street. "I can't take time off, Michelle. I wish I could, but I definitely can't tonight."

"Fine. But tonight has to be the last night. This baby is coming any minute."

"I just need to meet with one last key witness, and then I'll be home."

Michelle remained suspicious. "All right, Wes. Just keep your cell phone with you in case this baby makes a surprise visit."

Wesley pulled into their driveway. "I'll have it by my side all night."

"Promise me."

Wesley leaned over and kissed her on the cheek. "I promise you."

Michelle opened the door and struggled to exit the large vehicle.

Wesley jumped out of the driver's seat to assist her. "Don't forget to turn on the security alarm. I'll be home as soon as I can." He kissed her once again, this time on the lips.

Michelle remained silent as she left and waddled up the driveway to the house. Once she made it to the front door, Wesley re-entered the running vehicle, backed the car in reverse and squealed the tires on his way downtown.

CHAPTER 23

The Reunion

TUESDAY, OCTOBER 10, 2006
9:59 P.M.

Wesley walked down a long, dark staircase leading to a plain black door at the end of the landing. On the door hung a tiny hand-painted sign that read *Le Masquerade*. Wesley knocked on the door loudly, but no one answered it. He then turned the knob, noticing it was open, and entered a small room that looked like the reception area for Satan's dentist.

There standing at the tiny reception desk was a young, three-hundred-pound woman with bright green hair. She looked like a harpooned killer whale wearing a black and white spandex dress with barbs hanging through her eyebrows, nose, lips, chin and (presumably) her tongue. She studied Wesley closely, admiring his clean-cut good looks and athletic physique, licking her lips as if she would be eating a piece of his flesh for dinner. And given the bizarre nature of this place, the possibility was not entirely out of the question.

"First time here?" she asked.

"Yes."

"Are you a member?"

"No."

"Would you like to buy a membership?"

"No, I'm just here to meet someone."

"Well, you need to buy a membership to enter."

Wesley was annoyed. "Okay. How much is it?"

"Let's see, you're a single guy, right? Couples are cheaper. Lesbians are free."

Wesley was starting to lose his patience. "Yes, I am a single man."

"Then it's one-fifty for a twenty-four pass. Six hundred for the entire year."

"A hundred and fifty dollar cover fee?"

The green-haired goddess smiled. "Towels are near the locker room to the right. In case you want to fuck in the group hot tub."

Wesley was not impressed with Orca's answer. He pulled out his wallet, counted out one hundred and fifty dollars in cash, and then placed the money in front of her.

The green-haired goddess was impressed. "VIP rooms are extra, of course. Those run three hundred an hour plus tips."

"I won't be needing that."

"Are you sure? We've got the best girls in the South," she said in an infomercial voice. "Plus, tonight is our monthly two-for-one night in case you change your mind."

"No, thanks. I'm good." Truth was, Wesley *was not good*. He hadn't had sex in nearly three months and was about to burst like a snake out of his skin. The last thing he needed was to be in a strip club.

"Cool. You can go in now."

"Thanks." Wesley noticed a rainbow beaded curtain that looked like the entrance to a seventies nightclub. Just as he walked through it, a security alarm beeped softly.

"Whoops, sorry. No cameras, cell phones or any other electronics are allowed inside."

"But I need my phone. My wife is about to give birth."

The green-haired goddess gave him a look. "Then why are you here, *single dude?*"

Wesley begrudgingly took his cell phone out of his front pocket and handed it to her.

The green goddess smiled. "Thanks. Have fun."

As Wesley walked inside, the bass from the pounding house music entered his chest, rearranging the pattern of his heartbeat. To his surprise, the main nightclub was much larger than he'd expected, with an apocalyptic *Mad Max* décor, high tech lights, monolithic speakers, and small pub tables filled with cozy but ripped to shreds, high-back velvet chairs. As expected, he saw two strippers dancing on stage: identical twin redheaded sisters that were nude but covered with black fishnet body stockings. One was kissing and fondling the other, grinding her small pale fingers into the vaginal opening of her sister's body stocking as they danced to the music. The scene was sick, sexy and hot, making Wesley turn away to avoid making his personal matters any worse.

Instead, he examined the crowd surrounding him – gay, straight, black, white, yellow, brown – a rare sight indeed, especially in the South. Some of the club patrons were dressed in street clothes, others in thousand-dollar suits, and many more in leather and bondage gear. As soon as Wesley finished processing his surroundings, he realized that this was not a traditional gentlemen's club. No, sir, not at all. This place was something different. And whatever it was, he did not care to find out. For all he wanted was to find Ava and get the fuck out of there as soon as possible.

Wesley finally sat at a small empty table in the center of the room. And, as if the spirits were guiding him, it was the exact same table where his best friend, Sebastian O'Connor, sat moments before his death seven days ago.

Julie, the dirty, slow motion smack-head waitress from last week, arrived at Wesley's table wearing a see-thru black lace dress. But this time, she looked clean and smashing – like a gothic hooker back from the dead – with a new, short black bobbed hairstyle, a full face of make-up and a fresh set of needle tracks hidden by the tattooed sleeve on her arm.

"What would you like to drink?" she asked.

Wesley looked at her mid-section, noticing that her tattooed pussy and bare ass were on display for everyone in the room. "Do you have any Scotch?"

"Sure, we have, like, Jimmie Daniel, Jack Walker, Jim Beam, Wild Turkey and Southern Comfort...I think, like, that's it."

Wesley knew this girl was clueless. "I will have a Jack Daniel on the rocks. Make it a double." He spoke very slowly to her over the loud music.

"Okay." Julie left with her tray and wandered towards the back of the nightclub. While on her way, she stopped in the middle of the room, spoke to something invisible, then continued walking towards the main bar.

Wesley was uneasy and nervous waiting for his drink to arrive. He looked around the room, wondering if he could even remember what Ava looked like. He glanced at his Rolex: it was twelve minutes after ten. *Where the hell is she?*

Wesley looked at his Rolex one last time: it was now ten forty-five. With three double whiskeys in his system, he was drunk, angry and ready to leave. He rose from his seat, threw a hundred dollar bill on the table and prepared to leave the club.

Just then, a tall, glamorous woman dressed in a black, full-bodied catsuit sat down, slapping a pack of Marlborough Reds and a lighter on the table.

Wesley continued looking for the exit door, ignoring the sex worker before him. "I'm not buying anything to-night. Sorry."

"Not even a hello, Wesley? It's been such a long time."

He recognized the voice. But there was *no way in hell* he could recognize that face. *"Ava?"*

Her long, sleek, platinum blonde hair was now parted in the middle, gently gracing her perfectly sculpted, eighteenth century porcelain face. Her large woodsy-green eyes were now adorned with theatrical false eyelashes, reminiscent of a lioness hunting in the grass. Her body was perfect, long and lean as before, but now athletically toned and more resilient than ever. She was gorgeous. She was elegant. And she was the *sexiest woman* Wesley had ever seen.

"You look surprised to see me," she said.

Wesley nearly fell back into his seat. The shy, introverted book nerd he knew fifteen years ago was now a badass confident woman who wouldn't let God or Satan stand in her way.

"I just...I don't know. I didn't know what to expect."

Ava lit a cigarette as Wesley drooled. She took a long, sexy drag and blew it out.

"They patched me up rather well, wouldn't you say?"

Her comment reminded Wesley that this was *not* a friendly visit. "We're done. You realize that, don't you?

There's no more money. Not from me. Not from anyone in my family."

"Now what makes you think I want more money?"

Wesley was at a loss for words. "Then why the fuck did you visit my wife today?"

"I just wanted to say hello."

"Bullshit!"

A huge, Latino bouncer came to the table from nearby. "Is there a problem?"

"Oh, no, we're fine, Carlos. He's just an old friend from college." Ava's eyes sparkled as she looked at Wesley.

The bouncer shot him a dirty look then walked away.

As soon as it was clear, Ava leaned over the table, staring directly into Wesley's eyes. "I do want something from you, but it's not money."

He stared back at her. The sexual tension between them was instantaneous. After a few moments, she retreated back to her chair, took another drag from her cigarette and blew it out.

"Are you planning to tell me what you want or do we have to play games?"

"First we chat, then we play games."

Wesley couldn't decide if he wanted to strangle or fuck her.

Just then, Julie arrived with another drink.

"I didn't order a shot."

"I did. I assumed you still like Scotch," said Ava.

After serving the drink, Julie placed her tray on the floor and sat on Ava's lap like a child visiting Santa Claus at the mall.

"Julie, I want you to meet Wesley. He's the friend I've been telling you about."

He downed the Scotch in one shot.

Julie said nothing. Instead, she seductively pulled the cigarette out of Ava's mouth, took one long drag, and then carefully placed it back inside Ava's red lips.

There was no doubt in Wesley's mind: *these two are a tag-team.*

All he could think about from that point forward was watching the hot blonde stick her tongue inside the petite brunette. His cock was getting harder by the second.

"You should stick around until we get off work," suggested Ava.

He immediately began to feel woozy, his vision sway-ing as if he were on a boat.

"Did you drug me?" he slurred.

"Come home with us tonight."

Julie rose from Ava's lap, then straddled Wesley's left thigh...grinding her wet, decorated pussy on top of his leg while she kissed him.

Needless to say...Wesley *was toast.*

CHAPTER 24

You Lucky Bastard

WEDNESDAY, OCTOBER 11, 2006
12:14 A.M.

The girls walked on either side of Wesley, holding him upright through an exquisite brown and black marbled lobby. Wesley grinned at each beautiful lady by his side. "Y'all live in a nice building," he slurred.

"We should. I pay a shitload in dues," replied Ava.

Wesley smiled wide, thoroughly enjoying her dry sense of humor, almost as much as he enjoyed stroking her hot latex ass.

A middle-aged black man stood at the lobby desk in a maroon and gold uniform. "Good evening, Miss Ava. Miss Julie." He looked at Wesley with understandable envy. "Sir, I need you to sign in."

"Don't worry about him, Lucky, he's with us," replied Ava.

The doorman shot Wesley a *you-lucky-bastard* look. "All right, sir. You can go ahead. Have a good evening."

Wesley saluted him as the three exited the lobby and walked toward the elevator landing.

Inside the elevator, they stood apart like strangers.

Ava reached over and pushed the PH button.

"Does Julie ever talk?" he asked.

"No. She just fucks."

The elevator doors slammed shut.

Ava's two-story penthouse had the most spectacular views of the city, especially from the double terraces located on both the upper and lower floors. The entire place was magnificent, from the stunning yellow rose garden upstairs, to the black and white modern kitchen, living room and three guest bedrooms below. It was obvious Ava had done something extremely smart with her Scarborough money for a place like this cost well over ten million...A far cry from the twenty-dollar tips she earned as a dominatrix for hire.

Inside the master bedroom, Wesley's Thor-like naked physique stood at the edge of the bed, fucking Julie from behind. Her black lace dress pulled up around her waist, as she passionately kissed Ava beneath her.

Wesley stopped for a moment to whisper into Julie's ear. "Take her clothes off."

As they continued pressing their lips, Julie slowly unzipped Ava's black latex catsuit. After a while, Ava broke free to undress herself in front of Wesley. She pulled the front zipper down, all the way to the end of her pussy. She removed one shoulder at a time, revealing her porcelain neck, chest and waist underneath.

When she pulled down her entire top, Wesley saw only the most beautiful woman in the world...Her long platinum hair covering her breasts, her large eyes reflecting the waxing moon behind him, her full lips filled with the desire to suck his cock hard. Just then, he moved towards her, grabbing the rest of her catsuit at her waist, and pulled it down until a fully naked woman stood before him.

Now naked body to naked body, he reached for her breast hidden beneath her long hair, only to feel a strange line instead of a nipple. Confused, he moved her hair away to reveal two long, thick mastectomy scars standing where her nipples once were. Wesley gently kissed each of her missing breasts, refusing to remember how they came to be, and then put his tongue in her mouth as his finger gently touched her clit in swirling motions.

Julie moved behind him, cupping his balls and stroking his dick as he kissed Ava. Almost ready to cum, he broke free from the girls, and entered the bed on his back. Like a horny lioness, Ava climbed up and cornered him on all fours, with her perfect round ass high in the air, taking her tongue down his chest, to his stomach and around his balls. Finally, she took his large, hard cock fully in her mouth, and pleasured him wildly.

Julie, now fully naked, kneeled behind Ava as she did this, licking her ass then gently flicking Ava's small pink clit with the barb in her tongue, then back again.

From Wesley's point of view, watching Ava's long blonde hair caress his stomach as she sucked his cock – and Julie's short black hair buried in her ass behind her – was the hottest thing he had seen in a decade. The blood flowing to his groin was now mounting, and his resolve to last long enough to fuck the both of them was relentless.

He grabbed Ava's head from his dick and placed her face onto his, kissing her once fiercely. She then placed her pussy on top of him, riding him slowly...turning to kiss Julie while touching her pink clit buried inside a bouquet of illustrated flowers.

For him, the feeling of being inside Ava was like no other. She was so unusually tight and flowing with wetness – reborn by the Gods to be a sex machine for men and women alike. She was beyond hot. She was magical. And watching her long neck kiss and pleasure Julie made the feat of staying hard that much easier.

Wesley grabbed Ava by the hips and gently lifted her off him.

"I want to see you *fuck her*."

Ava moved over to Julie, both spreading their legs apart like two scissors interlocking their pussies, grinding one vulva to another…two wet cunts engaged in a French kiss. Ava then moved, placing her thumb onto Julie's clit while kissing and thrusting into her body.

Julie moaned with pleasure as Ava was the best lover she had ever known.

Wesley lay naked beside them, watching and not touching. His cock became stiffer and stiffer with every thrust. Ava then stopped for a moment and walked over to her nightstand. Julie sat up, smiling, knowing what was coming next. From the bottom drawer, Ava pulled out a black strappy pair of underwear, with a large, nude skin-colored dildo attached to the front. She stepped into the strap-on panty and climbed on top of Julie, placing the life-like cock inside her, fucking her missionary style.

Wesley could no longer handle it. He started touching himself while he watched.

Ava grunted, thrusting harder and harder into Julie as she moaned in pure delight. She kept fucking her and fucking her until she could tell Julie was about to cum... She then moved to spread Julie's thighs wide open, placing her warm tongue inside her burning hot pussy, making Julie squirm with delight.

Unable to take anymore, Wesley moved behind Ava, stuck his cock through the whole in the back of her strap-on, fucking her doggie style as she continued to lick and tease Julie's pussy. From this vantage point, he had a close look at the tattoo on Ava's back – a large black tribal phoenix rising from a city skyline below. His attention quickly turned back to Julie, who moaned until she reached her climax, cumming so loud with the balcony doors open that everyone on the floor could hear. Afterwards, she quietly laughed and rolled over, unable to stay awake or take any more pleasure for the night.

Wesley grabbed Ava's waist, pulling down her strap-on dildo, tossing her onto the bed beneath him. He climbed on top and continued to fuck her eye to eye.

Just then, their eyes locked. Their eroticism heightened beyond that physical moment in time. Wesley had always fought his feelings for Ava, but tonight he was ready to let go...Let go of his family, his friends, his entire past. In that moment, Ava was the *only soul* that did not judge him. And given her angelic ability to forgive, he felt like he could sink into her arms and be protected against the world forever.

Just as he was about to climax, words fell out of his mouth. "Ava, I'm in—"

Then just like that, he came – thrusting and bucking on top of her, coming harder and harder in waves, with his sperm bursting inside her while she gently caressed his messy dark blonde hair.

Finally, he was done.

"Ava," he said in heavy breath, looking deep into her reflective eyes.

"What, Wesley?" she whispered back.

His watery blue eyes said everything she suspected. "Ava, I think you're the only woman I ever—"

His cell phone RANG.

"Ignore it," she whispered, kissing him aggressively on the mouth. Wesley gave in to her passion, but as the phone continued to ring, reality came crashing down.

The baby.

He gently pulled away from her and stumbled out the bed. He bent over to the floor, naked, shuffling through his pants to find his phone.

He answered it out of breath. "Hello?"

"Where the hell are you? It's four thirty in the morning!" huffed Michelle.

"Jesus. I must have dozed off. I'm still at the office."

"You sound drunk."

"No, uh—"

"And why are you breathing so heavy?"

"I just ran down the hallway to get the phone. Why? What's the matter?"

"Well, I'm hurting like hell. I think I'm, in labor…"

"Are you still at the house?"

"Yes."

"I'm leaving right now. Just stay put until I get there."

Wesley hung up the phone, forgetting he was too drunk to drive home, let alone drive his pregnant wife to the hospital. He looked back to the bed and saw Ava was gone. But Julie was still there, naked and asleep on her side. For a second, he lost all focus and appreciated the outline of her small feminine body, especially her vine covered ass and well-adorned back. Julie was a youthful canvas of art indeed, one that strangely had the same phoenix back tattoo as Ava. And knowing what little he did about Julie, that powerful image of resiliency was actually a pitiful statement of irony on her.

Wesley looked out through the open terrace doors framed by white billowing curtains, and saw the city skyline buzzing behind it. It was cool and breezy now, and there stood Ava, in a short silk Kimono robe smoking a cigarette…her long, lean sweating body reflecting thousands of beads of light from the sky, each cell gazing at the stars above them.

Wesley walked outside, unsure of how to say goodbye.

"Listen, I have to go."

She spoke with her back turned to him. "You're in no shape to drive. I'll call a limo and have Lucky follow in your Escalade."

"Ava, I…I don't even know where to start. I don't…"

She turned around, with tears streaming down her face. "When can I see you again?"

Wesley was alarmed. "I don't know…honestly, I don't." He paused, thinking carefully before speaking the following words: "We can't do this, Ava. You realize that, don't you?"

"Why not?"

"Because we can't. This has to end. Tonight."

Ava's eyes showed how hard his words stung. She turned back around and continued smoking. "Just go then."

Wesley immediately regretted what he had said. "Ava, I'm sorry, I…"

Her face was taut and serious. "Please. Just go."

Wesley had no more words. He knew that what he had done that evening was quite possibly the most asshole thing in the history of assholes, so he just bowed his head and walked back inside. He grabbed his clothes from the floor and dressed himself as fast as he could.

When he finished, he noticed a video camera on a tripod in the corner of the bedroom. He looked outside to make sure Ava was not watching, then looked at the bed to make sure Julie was still asleep. He approached the camera, ejected the tape holder and saw that it was empty. *Whew*. Still unsure of what Ava wanted, at least now he knew it had nothing to do with money. And maybe, just maybe, Ava had received the type of closure she had been seeking all along.

CHAPTER 25

False Alarm

WEDNESDAY, OCTOBER 11, 2006
7:29 A.M.

Still wearing the same clothes as the night before, Wesley and Michelle silently entered their home. Wesley struggled for compassionate words. "I'm just as anxious as you are, Michelle. You heard the doctor, false alarms are completely normal."

She looked up at him with her sad, big brown eyes.

"What's the matter, baby?"

"You promised, Wes," she said with a crackled voice.

"Promised what, baby?"

Michelle started crying softly. "That you would stop cheating." She slowly waddled her way to the bedroom and closed the door behind her.

"What are you talking about?"

Confused, Wesley looked at his reflection in the foyer mirror and saw his red satin dress shirt was off by two buttons. "Goddammit."

———❦———

Wesley tried sleeping on his black sofa in the office, but the bright morning sun from the downtown skyline window was frying his face like a hot summer sidewalk. After flipping over several times, he finally took a large pillow and placed it over his head.

Lilly waltzed through the open office door, fresh and peppy as ever. "Wesley? What are you doing here? I thought your wife was in labor?"

Wesley replied under the pillow. "False alarm. Now go away."

"Get up. I've got good news."

"I need sleep, Lilly. I've been up all fucking night."

"Well did you catch the morning news?"

"I will die if I don't get some sleep."

"It's Sarah Vinson, Wesley. We won! She officially withdrew the charges this morning."

For a second, Wesley thought he was dreaming. He removed the pillow from his head and faced Lilly. "What did you say?"

"Saffroy is free and clear! All thanks to you...and me, and everybody else who works here of course."

"But...how?"

"I just told you, Sarah Vinson publically withdrew the charges at 8:00 A.M. She said she made the whole thing up because Saffroy ended their affair abruptly, and she was truly sorry. Now she's being charged with filing a false police report, but the DA said on TV he'll let her plea it out."

Wesley knew better. He'd *seen* the brutal rape on his own computer. "But why would she do that?"

"I guess she was tired of reading about herself in the papers."

Wesley shot her a look.

"What?"

"I fucking *hate* that saying."

"Why aren't you happy, Wes? Daniel Holt will give us a *huge* bonus. Christmas vacay money for everybody!"

The receptionist BUZZED on the intercom.

Wesley yelled back from the sofa: "What?"

"Mr. Scarborough, you have a guest up front. Would you like me to—"

"No. No visitors!" He placed the pillow back over his head.

"But it's an old friend from college."

Wesley sprung upright like a mousetrap. *Shit.*

"Lola, please do not let anyone back here. Tell her I'm in an important meeting with Lilly right now and that I'll give her a—"

David Reilly popped into Wesley's office. "Tell her what, man?"

Wesley rubbed his eyes raw. "Holy fuck, David?" Wesley fired off his sofa and they embraced like two old friends who hadn't seen each other in years.

"How the hell are you, good buddy?" asked Wesley.

Lilly smiled at the sweet reunion. She knew Ed had worked hard to find him.

"I heard you were looking for me, so I came by to see what the fuck you're up to these days," replied David, with a bird-eating grin on his face.

"I'll leave you two alone," said Lilly as she exited.

"I can't believe you're here, David. Sit down. Do you want a drink?"

"At nine in the morning?" David smiled. "Thanks, but I can't. I quit partying five years ago. NA is my dealer now."

Wesley was shocked. "Oh, wow, that's great...And you look great. Strong, healthy."

"Thanks."

"So where are you working now?'

"Deutsche Bank in London. Actually, I'm only back here to see the folks for like two days."

"Cool."

"Yeah, I'm here to pick up my mother's engagement ring so I can pop the question back in the UK."

"Holy shit, that's great, man. But you gotta catch me up over food 'cause I'm starving. Want to join me for breakfast?"

"Four Seasons?"

"Sure. Let's go."

—⚬⚬⚬—

Wesley and David sat at the busy Four Seasons restaurant, eating a table full of eggs, bacon, sausage, waffles, pancakes and rye toast. They ate like two starving children recently rescued from an abandoned ship. While they were feasting, an older waitress approached the table, refilling their coffees for the umpteenth time.

"The National Democratic Party? You're shitting me," said David, chewing on a piece of twenty-dollar French toast. "That's impossible."

"That's what I said."

"Now his family's broke?"

"*Dead broke.* They were already a half-a-million in the hole, so now Susie and the kids have to sell the house and move back to Tennessee with her mother."

"That sucks, man. I guess there's a lot we don't know about Sebastian…I mean, didn't know. Shit, I still can't believe he's fucking dead."

"Well, I just pretend he's away on a long business trip. That's how I cope with it."

"I hear ya, man."

"But you know, sometimes out of nowhere it does hit me hard…and I just want to bawl my fucking eyes out, you know?"

"I can imagine. Y'all were really close."

"Yes, we were."

"We *all* went through a lot of shit together."

Wesley faintly nodded in agreement, and then quickly changed the subject. "So, do you like London?"

"Hell no, it sucks. It rains all the fucking time, and the guys there dress like fags. Like half the straight men in my office wear hot pink and lavender French cuff shirts with suspenders and shit like that. Ridiculous. Plus all the EU liberals constantly bitch that America is fucking up the environment, everybody's starving in India and shit like that. It's a whole country full of pussies, man. They need to man up. Southern style."

"You can always move back here."

"Well, it's my girl. She's from there, so I'm probably gonna stay put."

"Yeah? Tell me about the future wife."

"Well, her name is Kylie. She's British, from Kent. Pretty hot I might add."

"Kylie Riley. Dig it."

"We live together now, and she's awesome. But the only thing giving me cold feet is the thought of having sex with the *same* woman for the rest of my life." David smiled. "Not like that's a problem for you."

"Not me, I'm through with that shit. I've got a baby coming any minute."

"Yeah, right." David leaned over the table. "Come on, man, tell me. How long have you been faithful this time?"

Wesley stared directly into David's eyes then looked at his Rolex. "Well, what time is it?"

"You fucker!"

"No man, but seriously. Last time, ever."

"Was she hot at least?"

Wesley hesitated.

"What? Stop holding back."

Wesley couldn't resist the urge. He reluctantly held up two fingers.

"Two women? Damn. I always wanted to be you in college, now I remember why."

The waitress interrupted their conversation with more coffee. "Can I get y'all something else?"

"No just the check, please," said David. "This one's on me."

As he was speaking, Wesley spotted Ava at the entrance of the restaurant. She was wearing a short, sexy, yellow raincoat and her signature large Jackie O' style sunglasses.

"Holy shit." Wesley partially ducked under the table. *Why does she fucking appear every time I think of her?*

"What? Who's behind me?"

"No one, uh, just a former client."

David turned around and zeroed in on an old man standing next to Ava.

"Who? The old geezer? Don't worry, he's leaving now. And so is the girl."

Wesley slowly lifted his face and looked at the entrance to confirm she had left.

"Damn, your client's daughter is fucking hot. Or was that his wife?"

"What?"

"The blonde in the yellow raincoat. I'd bang that bitch in a second."

Wesley shot him a look. "You know you're fucked in the head, right?"

David grinned. "I've missed you too, good buddy."

⸻ ⧂ ⸻

Outside, Wesley and David walked down a hilly sidewalk towards a tall parking garage across the street.

"Where are you parked?"

"Fourth floor I think. Do you need a ride back to the office?"

"No, man, it's a quick walk. I can use the fresh air."

"Cool."

Wesley gave him a big hug. "Hey, have a safe trip back and good luck with the proposal. I look forward to meeting Kylie at the wedding."

"Me too."

Wesley turned around and walked back up the hill towards his office.

"Hey, man, good luck with the diapers!" shouted David.

Wesley smiled, saluting him back. "You too!"

In the garage, David pulled a large tagged key out of his front pocket while walking along a dark, shaded floor. He walked towards a green Chevy Lumina in the distance. Just as he was approaching, the blonde woman in the yellow raincoat popped out from behind a shiny black conversion van with blocked out windows.

"Excuse me. I vas vondering if you could help," said Ava in her near-perfect Russian accent.

David recognized her as the hot chick from the restaurant. "Sure, how can I help you today?"

"My friend leave note on van and I not understand it very well." She took out a folded yellow piece of legal paper from her coat pocket and handed it to David.

"Sure, let's see here." He unfolded it and read it aloud, smiling. "I like it up the ass?"

BAM!!!

The van doors behind him swung wide open. Two bald, muscular bikers – one black and one white – jumped out. The black biker stuck a dirty rag into David's mouth as the other yanked him inside...Ava followed them all into the van and locked the doors behind her.

Inside, the black biker held David by the arms as the white one wrapped his trembling ragged-mouth with several rounds of duct tape. He then moved down David's body yanking off his dress pants, along with his dirty white Hanes underwear.

Ava stood directly over him. "How's London been treating you?"

David lay flat on the floor of the conversion van, fully nude from the waist down. His eyes shrieked pure fear, his body squirming and panicking, not understanding who these people were or why this was happening to him.

Ava took off her sunglasses and tilted her head to one side. "Oh, wait a second. You don't recognize me. I'm so sorry, David. It's Ava. Ava DeSantis."

David stopped squirming for two brief seconds then thrashed out harder than before.

"Oh, good. You do remember me now."

The bikers flipped him over onto all fours, placing his arms and legs in chains, with his hairy pale asshole exposed to the air.

Ava removed a pair of protective goggles and blue rubber gloves from her coat pocket and placed both items carefully on her body. She then tightened the belt on her yellow raincoat and bent over to examine his hairy asshole closely. "Oh my, you don't wipe very well. Disgusting."

Sweat rolled down David's brow, which combined with the spit running down his chin from silently screaming under the wads of duct tape around his mouth.

"Well, now that I know you like it up the ass, let's see what we can find here." Ava turned and grabbed a large golf umbrella from the floor. "How's this for starters?" She lunged the pointy end of the umbrella into his rectum, and hit the open button.

"AHHHHH!" David screamed through his home-made muzzle.

"That'll feel good here in a minute."

David moaned through his muzzle.

"What? Not yet?" Ava removed the umbrella, and lunged it again harder.

"AHHHHH!"

"Okay, that's done. Now let's see what else we have here." She picked up a rusty tire iron from the van floor. "Perfect"

She thrust the widest end of the tire iron, hard, cracking something inside.

David screamed wildly.

"Whoops. Did I hit a bone? Jeez, I hate when that happens."

David cried hysterically.

Ava glanced outside the one-way windows, confirming that no one was around. "Good. Looks like you're ready to go. Boys, who wants to go first?"

The big black biker unzipped his pants. He maneuvered behind David's ass and thrust his large cock inside of him. "You like fucking little girls?" he said through each thrust.

David wallowed silently.

"How does that feel, boy? You still like it up the ass?"

David's eyes crossed with pain.

The white biker gestured for the black one to step aside. "I've got this," he said in a low, deep voice.

As the black biker removed his huge black cock, fresh red blood ran out of David's asshole, gushing down his inner thigh. The rusty smell of blood mixed with shit filled the van, making the black biker gag as he moved away.

David's entire body shook waiting for the white biker to take his pants down to his ankles. He then positioned himself behind David, fucking the hell out him, pushing and cracking and pummeling his head into the van's exit doors in the back.

BAM! BAM! BAM!

In shock from the pain, David became limp and lifeless.

Ava rose from her seat and slapped David across the face. "Wake up, motherfucker. You're going to remember this day for the rest of your time in hell."

BAM! BAM! BAM!

David's eyes pleaded mercy, but Ava was enjoying every second of his long deserved punishment. The ass pounding continued for two long minutes until the white biker finally climaxed inside him...removing his dick, bloodied and soiled.

David was shivering on all fours, ass to the air, unsure of what was next. The smell of his wounds continued to fill the van: cum, shit, rust and blood, all wafting together in one small confined space. A smell so unique and horrific, one would remember it for a thousand lifetimes.

Ava tossed her silky, long blonde hair aside and continued with her speech. "What was your girlfriend's name again? Was it Kayla? Or Kendall?"

David shook his head at her violently.

"Kylie. That's right. Kylie Joy Watson."

"NOOOHH…" he murmured under the duct tape.

"Such sad news. Jumping from the Hornsey Lane Bridge like that. And she was what, only twenty-three years old?"

David broke down to pieces.

Ava moved in close to him. "My good friend tells me she was very distraught to hear how much you liked fucking six-year-old girls. Especially when he showed her all the kiddie porn pictures we put on your computer."

David became lifeless.

"Oh, don't give up so soon, David!" She slapped him on the back. "I have one more special treat for you. A blow job. Wouldn't you like that? One more great cock sucking before you die?"

David was terrified.

"Flip him over." The biker boys followed her orders. "Hold him tight."

David's entire body contorted in terror.

"Oh, look, a fear boner." David's average size, erect penis throbbed with adrenaline. Ava took off her shop goggles and pulled out a brand new filet knife from her raincoat pocket. She placed the edge of her knife to his scrotum and her tongue on his balls, licking them gently.

David shook like a prisoner about to be executed.

"Now stay still," she whispered. She took his fully erect cock into her mouth, sucking hard on his dick…But the more Ava's head bobbed up and down, the more his erection became softer and softer, dying down to almost nothing.

Ava lifted her head with surprise. "What's the matter? I don't turn you on anymore?"

David's eyes filled with incomprehensible terror. His penis was now limp, trembling in her presence.

"Well let's try this then."

Ava held up his limp penis with one hand as she cut the base of it off from his balls. David screamed and thrashed out in pain, as the bikers struggled to hold him. She then raised the bloody mass of penis flesh and placed it in her mouth, mimicking a blowjob in the air.

"How about now? Does this do it for ya?" she mumbled, with his bloody, severed penis in her mouth.

David's eyes closed slowly, for this was the last image burned into his memory before losing consciousness.

CHAPTER 26

BAD NEWS ALWAYS COMES IN THREES

WEDNESDAY, OCTOBER 11, 2006
1:41 P.M.

Wesley sat at his desk staring at the city skyline, thinking of ways to win back Michelle's trust. *Baby, we all went to a nightclub to blow off some steam (yes, that would explain the drinking) and, believe it or not, there were these two old ladies who started dancing with me, so as a joke, I unbuttoned my...*

Lilly tiptoed in. "Wesley?"

"Whatever it is, I don't want to know about it."

Lilly did not move. Her labored breath was enough to get Wesley's attention.

He turned around in his chair. "All right. What is it?"

"Your friend...the one that came in here this morning."

"David Reilly? What about him."

Lilly hesitated. "Well, it's all over the police wire, Wes. I am so sorry."

Wesley hunched over his desk. "*What* is all over the police wire?"

Lilly braced herself for his reaction.

"What, Lilly? Tell me!"

Lilly looked at the floor as she spoke. "David was murdered this morning. He was attacked in his rental car and bled to death."

"Wait, are you sure it's the same David Reilly? I was just with him a few hours ago."

"I know."

"Where did this happen?"

"The parking garage down the street."

Wesley covered his head with his elbows. Lilly approached him, having no idea how to comfort someone who had just lost two friends in eight days. "Wesley, I—"

Wesley blurted into Lilly's face. "What time? What time did they find him?"

"I, I, I don't know. All I know is that they found a picture of a naked little girl pinned to his shirt. It was a very young girl…which is why first responders think it may have been some sort of hit relating to child molestation."

Wesley melted in his chair.

"But they won't know anything until the autopsy is finished. That's all I know. I swear."

Wesley jumped to his feet and paced around his office like a madman. "This is not happening, this is not happening…It's just not happening…"

"I don't know what to say, Wes. I am *so* sorry."

"Something is going on here…something is going on…"

"Wesley, calm down. I can drive you home. Just take it easy."

"No! There's something going on!"

"Wesley please—"

"First Sebastian, now David. Then that bitch comes out of nowhere…" Wesley stopped in his tracks, looking straight ahead. "Oh, my God."

Lilly was frightened. "I don't understand."

"What was the name of the place where they found Sebastian?"

Lilly thought hard. "Something like…"

"It was a sex club, right?"

"Yes, it was called something like *The Mardi Gras*?"

"Was it *Le Masquerade*?"

"Yes, that's it!"

Wesley's stomach fell to the floor. He became dizzy, almost falling over. Lilly grabbed his arm then swiped his keys off the desk.

"That's it. I'm taking you home."

With a belly now ready to burst, Michelle escorted Lilly outside of her home. Her oversized white sweater with black sequin bats made her look like an overfilled Halloween trick or treat bag. "Thank you so much for driving the Escalade here too, Lilly. It saves me from having to go back downtown twice in one day."

A yellow cab pulled into the driveway and beeped the horn.

"There's my ride. Oh, and please tell Wesley I'll take care of everything at work so he can take a few day off and sleep. Just please, *make* him sleep."

Michelle smiled. "I'll make sure he gets plenty of rest. Thanks again."

Inside, Wesley lay curled up in his bed, staring blankly at the wall before him. Michelle entered the room, doing her best to cheer him up. "Hey, are you awake?"

Wesley did not respond.

"Well, I've been thinking, and you know all that stuff from this morning? Just forget about it. I'm sure your hair was just messed up from sleeping at the office, baby. I'm not mad anymore."

Wesley held onto the pillow, not saying a word.

"Oh, and I finally opened that gift basket today. Can you believe there was a bottle of Opus and a can of Beluga in there? How silly of me to wait."

Wesley ignored her, unable to think of Ava and her tricks any longer.

"Oh, and guess what else was in there?" Michelle grabbed something large and held it up in the air. "Check it out...Come on, look at me, Wes!"

Wesley reluctantly rolled over to see Michelle holding up a pink fifties diner style uniform – the one Ava wore the night of the rape. "Cute, right? It's almost my size. I think I can fit into it by Halloween."

Wesley rolled back over, not saying a single word.

———— ✲ ————

Michelle was making a peanut butter and jelly sandwich in the kitchen while talking on the phone. "I didn't realize David was such a close friend. I never met him."

"He wasn't really, in fact, I haven't heard his name in years. All I recall is that they went through some tough classes together in college. History class I believe," said Miriam on the other line.

Michelle served herself a glass of milk. "Oh...I wonder why Wesley's so upset then? He's practically catatonic."

"He's just exhausted from working too hard, sugar. Plus he's stressed out about becoming a father any day now. All to be expected, nothing to worry about."

"How soon can you get here?"

"I'm leaving Alpharetta right now but I need to stop and get some chicken soup."

Michelle looked inside a cabinet. "Oh, no, you don't need to stop. I've got four cans right here."

"But you never purchase the brand he likes, sugar. I'll stop by Kroger and get some."

Michelle's eyes darkened. "Okay, Miriam. Whatever you say."

Miriam exited Kroger grocery store, walking quickly through the parking lot shaded by an overcast sky. She was juggling two brown paper bags against her lavender Chanel suit, never once taking a breath while rambling into her cell phone. "No, Mary, everything's fine, Wesley just needs to stop working so hard and face reality, I already know this baby will require all of *his* attention because Miss Trailer Park America has no idea what she's doing." Miriam reached for her quilted purse. "Shoot! Darn it, I left my car keys at the cash register, I'll call you back later." Miriam leaned the bags of groceries against the rear tire of a white Mercedes S Class and headed back towards the store…

While Ava watched the entire scene from afar.

Miriam drove her white Mercedes down State Road 400, singing along to Carrie Underwood's *Jesus Take The Wheel* on the radio. Her heavily made up light blue eyes matched her over-teased bleach blonde hair that was so big it graced the headliner.

Suddenly, she felt something wrong with the steering.

BOOM!!!

Miriam's back tire blew out. She swerved left, almost hitting a pickup truck and then right nearly crashing into a Volvo. Eventually she pulled over safely to the side of the road.

As she sat recovering from the ordeal, she heard the rumbling sound of Ava's yellow Lambo pulling up right behind her. Miriam looked directly into the rear view mirror, recognizing the familiar sports car. "You never give up, Miss DeSantis, do you?"

Ava SPRUNG UP from the backseat. "No, I don't."

She threw a thick rope over Miriam's head, pinning her neck to the headrest, choking her.

Miriam started flailing and fighting, grabbing at the rope as hard as she could...but Ava was stronger, tying the rope several times in knots at the back of the headrest.

Miriam kept gurgling and mumbling under The Home Depot clearance death brace. "You'll...never get away..." she gargled. "I'll tell...the police...everything."

"Good point." Ava stuck her fingers into Miriam's mouth, yanked her tongue out and sliced it off with the filet knife. She rolled down the window and threw the pink tongue into the fast-moving traffic.

Miriam stretched her eyes to watch in horror as speeding cars rolled over it, flattening it to nothing. She continued to scream for help, now sounding like a deaf person trying to speak for the very first time.

"What was that again, Miriam? Tell the police, what?"

Miriam screamed as loudly as she could, yet no one on the road could hear her over the whizzing sound of fast-moving cars. Ironically, no one saw her either – all eyes were focused on the kick-ass yellow Lamborghini parked behind her instead.

"Give it a rest, Miriam. Enjoy a little peace before you burn in hell."

Miriam continued screaming, flailing, mouthing words and making noises, with her neck strangling and blood gushing from her mouth.

Okay, I'll hurry this up. Ava pulled out a large can of lighter fluid from the backseat. She dumped it all over Miriam's big blonde hair, then over her stretched out face, padded shoulders and blood-covered chest. Miriam spit out the lighter fluid, screaming and carrying on incessantly. "AHHHHHH!"

Yes, even without a tongue, Miriam Scarborough would not shut the fuck up.

I should've brought a gun. Ava finished dumping the lighter fluid on Miriam then exited the backseat of the car.

Outside, Ava stood with her back against the traffic, wearing her iconic yellow raincoat. Miriam continued to squirm, spit and scream. Her neck merged with the imported camel leather headrest, while Ava calmly pulled out her cigarettes and lighter.

Miriam stopped screaming. Her eyes were as wide as Texas.

"I know, I know, smoking makes me age faster." Ava lit the cigarette, took one long cinematic drag and blew out the smoke like a 1930s glamor queen. She then tossed the cigarette through the open window and into Miriam's flammable lap.

"There. I quit."

Miriam thrashed like a witch about to burn at the stake.

Ava calmly walked back to her car parked behind them. She opened the passenger door and dropped down into the seat.

"Feeling any better?" asked the bald, white biker in the driver's seat.

"Almost." Ava smiled with a sparkle of sarcasm in her eyes.

"Hey, any excuse to drive your car, boss."

"Just don't get used to it."

The biker grinned as he REVVED the engine. He hit the gas, darted into the stream of rushing cars and sped off into the distance...

Just then, the interior of Miriam's car burst into flames.

CHAPTER 27

Burn Baby Burn!

THURSDAY, OCTOBER 12, 2006
6:35 A.M.

Miriam lay semi-unconscious in her private hospital room at the Grady Burn Center. She looked like a dead papier-mâché spider with her arms and legs held up in the air by cables, and her face and body wrapped head to toe in pristine white gauze. The sound of her breathing tube and heart monitor filled the sterile room as Wesley and Thomas sat at her bedside wearing white protective clothing to prevent further infection.

"When were you planning to tell me?" asked Wesley.

"I wanted to tell you as soon as the decision was made, but your mother insisted we wait until the baby arrived. She was afraid it would cause you too much stress."

"Too much stress?"

"It doesn't matter now."

Thomas looked at Miriam with unconditional love in his eyes. "I just don't know what kind of monster could do this, Wesley. I know we risk our lives every day working in the legal system. I just always thought something like this would happen to me, not her."

"I know." Wesley was uneasy in his chair. He could not bring himself to tell his father the truth about who he suspected was behind the attack.

"She's the one who *defends* these monsters...and she's good to them. She understands them...I just don't know why anyone would turn on her like this."

Wesley slouched back in his chair out of sheer exhaustion. "All we can do is pray she'll wake up and be able to identify the attackers. That's all we can do."

Thomas looked at Miriam with tears in his eyes. "I don't know what I'll do if she doesn't make it, Wesley. As much as we fought, she's been by my side for nearly forty years." He stood up from his chair and held her hand. "It can't end like this. Not like this."

Wesley rose from his seat to comfort him. After a few moments, he launched a missile of unpleasant reality. "You do realize we have another serious problem on our hands, don't you?"

"The press?"

"Yes."

Thomas sighed. "How much time do I have?'

"My guess is that the story will hit by this afternoon."

Thomas looked at the floor, defeated.

Wesley grabbed Thomas by his wide, stately shoulders. "Hey, I promise you that I will do everything in my power to make sure the world knows you're innocent of this." Thomas looked away, unconvinced. "This is what I do best, Dad. I will take care of you, I promise."

Thomas drew a deep breath, ready for the worst to be over.

"All right then, son. Just tell me what I need to do."

CHAPTER 28

The Spin Of Innocence

THURSDAY, OCTOBER 12, 2006
5:07 P.M.

The ScarCom Gang assembled around the conference room table watching the local news broadcast on a flat screen television hanging in the corner. All of the ladies were eagerly rearranging their pens and paper while Derek and Ed munched on sub sandwiches they'd had delivered minutes earlier.

Wesley, now freshly showered and shaved, glared at the men from the head of the table, mindful that everyone else had worked straight through lunch earlier in the day.

"Sorry," said Ed with a piece of bread in his mouth. He quickly placed the sandwich back in the wrapper. Derek, oblivious to Wesley's disapproval, continued stuffing his mouth until Ed nudged him under the table.

A young black female news anchor took center frame on the television. "Thanks, John. We wish the students of Georgia Tech a fast and speedy recovery. Another major tragedy today involving fire—"

"All right. Here we go."

"Miriam Scarborough, local criminal defense attorney and wife of United States District Court Judge Thomas J. Scarborough, remains in critical condition this evening as the result of a mysterious arson attack on State Road 400 yesterday afternoon. Although no witnesses have come forward, police are asking the public to share any information they may have—"

The channel flipped...

"With a stellar record on violent crime, The Honorable Thomas J. Scarborough submitted his resignation at two o'clock this afternoon after serving nearly four decades on the bench—"

The channel flipped...

"One member of Miriam Scarborough's legal team has confirmed to Fox 5 that she had begun proceedings to divorce her husband of thirty-seven years, Judge Thomas J. Scarborough. When we asked our source if he thought it was a possibility Judge Scarborough might be involved in the attack, he said, and I quote, 'Miriam is tough as nails. I can't imagine anyone willing to take her on—"

The channel flipped...

"Thomas Scarborough, who's inherited net worth is estimated around two hundred million dollars, is expected to be officially named as a suspect by the police later this week."

Unable to tolerate any more, Wesley turned off the television. He silently rose from his chair, grasping at the remote control. His legendary slick blonde hair, blue eyes and bright smile were all fading into a gray ghost version of himself.

"What's our plan?" he asked.

The ScarCom gang looked at one another around the room.

"We need to pound the airwaves hard," said Loretta, the middle-aged black woman.

"What's the spin?" asked Derek.

"The spin is that my father is innocent," replied Wesley. "He *is* innocent. I know it without a doubt."

Amoli raised her hand. "But, sir, how do we leak *that*?"

Wesley fumed at her question as the receptionist entered the room.

"Mr. Scarborough, Detective Zhao is here to see you."

The room was quiet. The gravity of the case was finally hitting home.

"Please seat him in my office. I'll be right there."

⸎

Detective Rudy Zhao (rhymes with *Pow!*) was a slim, cocky Chinese cop in his early fifties. His wide collared shirt, spiky black hair and dimpled cheeks made him look like a disposable bad guy straight out of a Bruce Lee movie. Yet his interest in being a good guy came at the age of thirteen (just a few years after his parents emigrated from Hong Kong) when his father was mugged and stabbed while closing their College Park convenience store for the night. Fortunately, his father survived, but the homeless assailant was never found, something that still burns Zhao to this day.

Wesley entered his office in a hurry. "Sorry to keep you waiting."

Zhao was slouched down in a client chair, casually drinking a Corona beer. "No problem," he said in his mild Chinese accent. "I really dig the whole retro 'bar at the office' thing by the way. I hope you don't mind, I went ahead and helped myself."

"Not at all, that's what it's there for. I'm Wesley Scarborough."

"Detective Rudy Zhao." They shook hands. "I'm sorry we are meeting under these circumstances."

"Thank you." Wesley looked at the empty chair beside Zhao. "Should we be expecting someone else?"

"Oh, you mean my partner?" He laughed. "That's only in the movies, Mr. Scarborough. Not in Hotlanta. We're in the running for number one murder capital *again* this year…Way too many cases and not enough detectives to work them."

"Yes, I read about that."

"In fact, forensics is hiring butchers from Winn-Dixie to keep up, so if you know of anyone looking for work, let me know."

Wesley smiled awkwardly.

Zhao cleared his throat and continued. "Okay, so I did some research on you before I came here. You were the guy that defended the lawyer in that stripper rape case. Safflower wasn't it?"

"Saffroy. Jacob Saffroy. Yes, I was the spokesperson for his law firm."

Zhao shook his head. "See, *that* is a perfect example of why I left sexual assault years ago. Can't stand the 'he said, she said' shit."

"I can relate." Wesley shifted his weight.

"Funny how a woman would risk exposing her hooker past just to get back at a married man who dumped her?"

"Stranger things have happened."

"Yes, they certainly have." Zhao finished his beer then placed the empty bottle on the steel desk. Wesley was eager to jump in.

"Let me save you some time, Detective Zhao. My father had nothing to do with this."

"With all due respect, Wesley — I can call you Wesley, okay?"

"Yes."

"Unfortunately, your mother was entitled to one hundred million dollars in the event of a divorce. That's a hell of a lot of money to lose. Shit, I'd whack *my* wife for that kind of cash and she gives great head."

"No, you don't understand. There's someone else who's responsible for this." He leaned across his desk. "I know who tried to kill my mother."

"Uh-oh, I feel a story coming. Do you mind if I get another beer first?"

Wesley went to the bar, annoyed. "What would you like?"

"I see you already ran out of malt liquor so why not give me something rich white people drink."

Wesley handed him a green bottle of Heineken beer.

"Thank you. Now you can go ahead with your story."

Wesley drew a deep breath. "Detective, two of my best friends were murdered recently and now my mother was attacked. I believe the same person is responsible for all three events."

"Interesting. Sounds like *you* might have pissed someone off."

Wesley ignored his smug response. "Back in college, my two roommates and I partied with this nerdy, awkward girl one evening. She was over at our house to help us study for a big history exam, and we all winded up drinking way too much alcohol. Then, one thing led to another, and we had sex. All four of us."

Zhao placed his hands behind his head and kicked his feet onto the desk. "*Now* you've got my attention. Please continue."

"Unfortunately, this girl became pregnant. She didn't know which one of us was the father so she threatened to have the baby if we didn't give her money. She kept calling and hounding us to help her, and when we didn't, she turned into a complete psycho."

"I see. Psycho girl blackmails rich boys."

"Yes, and she kept threatening us until my mother stepped in and paid her to have an abortion...and she did, but..."

"Buuuut? Whaaat?"

"The girl lost her ability to have children as a result."

"Okay, well, that's a zinger. So let me see if I got this right: you all gang-bang psycho chick, she gets knocked up, blackmails your parents, has botched abortion, loses her plumbing and asks for more money?"

"Yes, and we gave her more money. It was a simple, financial transaction between two consulting adults."

"You mean four consenting adults. How much did your mother give her?"

Wesley hesitated. "I'm not sure. She handled that part."

Zhao removed his feet from the desk. "Sounds plausible so far, Mr. Wesley, except for one thing. How did your mother know the baby was yours?"

"Excuse me?"

"I mean, if it was a crackerjack orgy, then why was *your* mother the one to pay her off? Not your friends' families? Shouldn't everyone have chipped in like a potluck payoff?"

"Because my mother wanted to keep everything quiet."

"Really?"

Wesley leaned in closely. "Detective Zhao, my family had the most to lose at the time, and it still does. My mother didn't even tell my father about it. She said he would never forgive me."

"Why not? Sons knock up crazy girls all the time."

"Because he's a judge. And he doesn't forgive anyone. Ever."

"I see. But you all have been out of college, what, how many years now?"

"Fifteen, I think."

"So why would psycho girl come back *now* to start taking you all out?"

"I don't know. That's what I haven't figured out yet."

Zhao plucked a piece of paper and pen from Wesley's desk. "What information do you have on psycho girl?"

"Well, I know her name is Ava DeSantis—"

Zhao shook his head. "I don't know why, but that name sounds familiar to me. Is she a soap opera actress or something?"

"No, not that I know of."

"Hmm. I love those damn shows. Come one o'clock, everyone fights for the remote in the break room." Zhao wrote something down. "Okay. Go on. What else do you know?"

"She's originally from Atlantic City."

"Yes, Jersey girls, very tough. Hard to get brains out of hairspray that thick."

Wesley was stoic.

"Okay. Do you know where she lives now?"

"Yes, somewhere here. In a Midtown high-rise, I believe."

"And how do you know that?"

"I just heard rumors."

Zhao wrote something down. "Anything else?"

"Yes, she works at a place downtown called *Le Masquerade*. That's the sex club where they found my friend, Sebastian O'Connor last week."

"Oh, the guy with the dog collar? That's who you mean? Oh, hell, we had so much fun with that one.

All day people were barking like dogs and wanking off around—"

Wesley glared at him.

"All right. I'll make some calls up north and check out this girl, but in the meantime, don't let your father get too comfortable. I'm not done with him yet."

"Yes, sir. I understand. I just need you to protect my wife from this woman. She's very pregnant and Ava has already...I mean, she's crazy. I'm afraid she will hurt my wife."

"I'll try to get a patrol car to watch your house, but I can't guarantee it."

"Fair enough."

Zhao rose from his chair and headed for the door. On his way, he paused and turned back to Wesley. "I forgot to ask you one question."

"Yes?"

"How come you're not worried that psycho girl will come after *you*?"

"I am. I am worried."

Zhao cocked his head. "You sure don't look like you're worried. But then again, I guess that's why you make the big bucks. Nerves of steel."

"Yes, that's right."

"Okay. I'll be back in touch very soon."

"Thank you, Detective. I really appreciate your help."

Zhao acknowledged his comment then exited his office. Seconds after he was gone, Wesley fell back in his chair and exhaled.

CHAPTER 29

Visiting Hours

THURSDAY, OCTOBER 12, 2006
7:37 P.M.

Grady Hospital was unusually busy that evening. The five-alarm apartment fire at Georgia Tech had created so much chaos in the burn center that Thomas and Michelle had decided to go home early after a long visit with Miriam, who was now awake but still unable to speak or move. Hospital workers were scattered throughout the Intensive Care Unit, hustling from room to room; grieving parents were lined up in the hallways consoling one another; and mascara stained co-eds roamed the corridors making sure each Yellow Jacket BFF was like, okay.

Ava pranced down the busy hallway wearing a brown wig, child-like pink dress, and a stuffed pregnant belly, while carrying a ridiculously large bouquet of long-stem yellow roses. She waltzed right into Miriam's hospital room, completely unnoticed by the busy staff, as bouncy and peppy as a kid starting the first day of school.

"Hey, Miriam! Wake up!" she said in a loud voice, mocking Michelle's South Georgia accent. "It's Ava. Wesley's wife."

Miriam's face was between gauze dressings and open to the air. She looked like *Burn Victim Barbie* with remnants of blonde strands of hair popping out from various places on her scorched scalp. Her distinctive cheekbones were now fat and swollen, her radiant skin now charred black and oozing a greenish substance, her large accordion plastic breathing tube was still attached to her mouth and shoved down her throat. She slowly opened her melted blue eyes as Ava placed the large flower arrangement beside her on the nightstand.

Ava overreacted to her disfigured face. "My goodness, you look like shit, Miriam! I wonder if you can get a refund on all that expensive plastic surgery."

Miriam struggled to lift her melted eyelids wider. Once she realized who was speaking, her body twitched in response, but the cables kept her from moving.

Ava smiled at the grotesque scene in front of her. "You know, Miriam, from the bottom of my heart, I do not judge you in anyway. Wesley tells me that you are a very nice mother, and what you do behind closed doors in no way affects my opinion of you." As she spoke, Ava removed a large container of Morton Salt from her purse and opened the top.

The sound of Miriam's heart monitor started to climb.

"But it's very important that this little mishap stays between us."

Miriam's squinty blue eyes screamed for help, her mouth unable to move, bound to the breathing tube by plastic medical tape.

Ava shook the free flowing container of salt onto Miriam's head and face. "I'm afraid, that since your family is so well known around here that if you tell your story to anyone, it will surely make the headlines."

Miriam cringed from the intense pain.

Ava continued pouring the salt as she spoke. "Do you really want everyone to know this happened to you, Miriam? Do you really want to read about yourself in the papers, Miriam? I would hate to see you ruin your entire life for just one little mistake. Miriam."

The stinging pain of the salt was so unbearable, she jerked within her soul.

Once Ava was done pouring, she placed the empty container back into her purse.

"Wait, I almost forgot! I have a present for you!" Ava removed a handheld DVD player and placed it on Miriam's food tray table.

She hit PLAY.

The sounds of sex filled the room. "Oooh. I bet all Scarborough men are good in bed. All that blue blood filling up their big cocks."

Miriam closed her eyes.

"Now, come on, Miriam. Open your eyes!" Ava yanked the full bedpan from underneath her torso and dumped urine all over her face.

Unable to move or react, Miriam forced her eyes shut as the stinging urine splashed her face, melting the salt even more...Her body trembled, reacting to the intense cutting pain.

The DVD continued to play...

"Oh, I bet you're wondering who that is. That's Julie, my girlfriend. She's just a runaway junkie with a brain tumor, but that's a *whole* different tragic story."

Miriam grimaced, still refusing to watch the video but unable to avoid hearing it.

"Wesley really enjoys fucking her. Almost as much as he does me."

Miriam's soul began melting inside.

"Oh, and for the great news! The doctors were wrong, Miriam. I *can* have a baby!"

Ava pulled back and showed Miriam her pregnant belly.

"In fact, I'm due this week."

Miriam cracked her eyes open one last time, looking at Ava straight on.

"I'm thinking about changing my last name to Scarborough. What do you think?"

And with those words, Miriam finally gave up her struggle. The heart monitor halted to a flat line, setting off the alarm...as her burnt body finally relaxed into peace.

"That's what I thought." Ava quickly grabbed the DVD player and put it back in her purse. She walked casually out of the room, down the busy hallway, passing hospital workers as they rushed in the opposite direction.

CHAPTER 30

The Final Countdown

FRIDAY, OCTOBER 13, 2006
3:14 P.M.

Detective Zhao stood impatiently on the bright sunny doorstep of the Scarborough Mansion. For a third time, he smashed the gold lion knocker guarding the red double doors.

Miss Eloise – almost unrecognizable in her black velvet dress and coordinating birdcage fascinator – finally answered the heavy door. "Good afternoon, sir. Can I help you?"

Zhao flashed his badge. "I need to speak with Wesley, please."

Miss Eloise stepped partially outside. "Sir, he just cremated his mother this morning. Is there any way this can wait?"

"No, ma'am, it can't. I'm sorry."

She nodded and let Zhao into the lavish home.

Inside, at least sixty gray and black figures gathered in the echoing marble foyer. Thomas, Wesley and

Michelle stood near the banquet table receiving condolences from Miriam's vast network of friends: prominent attorneys, lifetime church-addicts and the slimeball Wall Street criminals whom she had once proudly called clients.

Wesley immediately spotted Zhao and approached him. "Did you find anything?"

"Yes. But we need to talk...alone."

"Sure, we can go into the library. Follow me."

Zhao grabbed his shoulder. "No, not here. Let's go out and grab a beer."

"Now? But, Detective, my wife—"

Michelle interrupted. "Go with him. I'll be fine."

"Are you sure?"

"Yes, of course."

Wesley mulled it over, then handed his car keys to Michelle. "If you get home before I do, put the security alarm on. First thing."

"Okay."

"I mean it, Michelle. This is very serious."

"Yes, I know."

"And if anyone tries to break in, you know where the gun is?"

"Yes. You showed me a dozen times."

"Good." Wesley kissed her on the forehead. "I'll be home shortly."

"So when are you due, Mrs. Scarborough?" asked Zhao.

"Today," she said sadly.

Zhao's expression couldn't hide his thoughts: *what shitty timing.*

Wesley grabbed a tweed coat out of the front closet. "Let's go. I can't take any more of this funeral shit."

———

Wesley and Zhao parked themselves at the bar inside Mister Wok's upscale Chinese restaurant. Two empty bottles of Tsingtao beer stood before them.

"Yes, psycho girl is a real piece of work, Wesley," he finished slugging his second beer. You sure know how to pick them."

"With all due respect, Detective, is there *any way* we can just stick to the facts tonight? I'm, I'm at my breaking point. This is definitely the worst day of my life."

Zhao whipped out his notebook, completely ignoring Wesley's request for mercy. "Like you asked, I ran both federal and state background checks on psycho girl. And it looks like she's been very busy."

"In what way?"

"Over the past decade alone she's been arrested on four counts of solicitation, three counts of possession, two DUI's and pro-bation in a pear tree."

Wesley was unmoved.

"I also called one of my former colleagues who moved to vice in Atlantic City. He told me that psycho girl was a very popular streetwalker who worked the convention center circuit for years. Beautiful girl, except she had a nasty heroin habit that kept getting her busted."

"Really? *Heroin?*"

"Yes. And he told me that cops up there nicknamed her 'brains' because she would ask for a crossword puzzle every time she went into a holding cell. Very smart girl. Why she became a hooker is what intrigues me."

Wesley's chiseled face remained indifferent. "What else did you find?"

"We also checked your mother's personal bank records like you suggested. You were right. She made two wire transfers to a brokerage account owned by Nick DeSantis in Atlantic City. One was in February 1991 for half-a-million dollars and the other was for the exact same amount, fifteen years later, practically to the day."

"Okay."

Zhao's demeanor changed. "Wesley, your mother paid Ava one million dollars to have an abortion."

"Yes, I understand that."

"Don't you think that's a bit steep? Eighteen years of child support wouldn't have added up to that much money."

"Well, I—"

"Wesley, there's a piece of information missing here. And my bet is that you're the *only one left* who knows it. Think hard. What am I overlooking?"

A fog of silence suddenly filled the bar...

Wesley had finally run out of stories.

Meanwhile, Michelle drove their black Escalade down Birchwood Road, approaching her home in the distance.

She spotted Ava jogging on the sidewalk, decked out in sexy black yoga pants and a yellow hooded sweatshirt.

Michelle pulled alongside her. "Hey, Ava!"

Ava waved and turned on her best Southern twang. "Hey, Michelle. How are ya?"

Michelle's big brown eyes welled with tears.

"What's wrong, honey?"

"Everything."

Ava casually looked around to see if anyone was watching. "Want some company? I'm tired of running anyways."

"Sure, why not. Hop in."

Wesley began sweating under his sleek, black Versace shirt.

"What's even stranger is that Nick DeSantis committed suicide *the same night* the second wire transfer was made. Isn't that odd?"

"What? Ava's father is dead?"

"Yes. And here I was thinking this was going to be some boring investigation of a bunch of spoiled *gwai lo*."

Wesley ignored the insult. "What happened?"

"According to the police report," Detective Zhao referred to his notebook. "Nick took a gym bag full of cash to the Trump Taj Mahal, which was the hotel where Ava was living at the time. He knocked on the door, handed her the money, told her how sorry he was for quote 'destroying her life' then stuck a .44 caliber in his mouth and blew his brains out right in the hallway...right in front of psycho girl."

"Oh my God. That's horrible."

"You bet it is. And when the police arrived, she turned the bag of cash over to them and said *she had no idea* where he got it. Two days later, she checked into Ocean County Rehab for Women, and when she was out, she booked a first class flight to Atlanta Hartsfield. That's it. Clean record ever since."

"So she's sober now?"

"Appears so."

"And unemployed?"

Zhao hesitated. "Well, she hasn't paid taxes since 1991."

"Then *how the hell* did she get so much money?"

"What do you mean?"

"Her condo, her car. If she blew the first payment on drugs and didn't keep the money from the second payment, then how did she become so wealthy?"

"There's lots of ways to get rich, Wesley. Maybe she's *dealing* the smack now. Or maybe she's milking rich ass sugar daddies – or in her case, sugar *mommas* – who the hell knows. All I know is that I wasn't able to find any property or cars registered in her name."

"Wow. She must blame all of us for her father's death."

"Yes, could be a motive."

Wesley raked his hand through his dark blonde hair. "Can you excuse me? I need to call my wife and make sure she's okay."

"Certainly, please do so."

Zhao turned to the bartender and in Chinese, ordered another round.

Michelle served Ava a second glass of sweet iced tea.

"Perfect. Thanks."

The pressure of her son's impending birth, combined with her mother-in-law's recent death, was finally taking a toll on Michelle's spirit. Her eyes were sallow, her body bloated, her energy listless. "I feel like I'm losing my mind," she said in a solemn tone.

"You need to take some time for yourself, Michelle. Relax. Take a spa day before your son arrives." Ava inconspicuously grabbed a large object in the front pocket of her sweatshirt. "You need to recover from this ordeal."

"I'm trying."

Ava's large green eyes perked as she took another sip of the delicious tea. "How's your husband holding up? He was close to his mother, right?"

Michelle cocked her head. "He's not doing well. None of us are handling this well…" She walked over to the junk drawer. "Especially me."

With Michelle's back turned, Ava slowly rose and approached her…her hand gripping the large object in her sweatshirt…waiting…ready to make her move…

Suddenly, Michelle turned around. "I know who you are, Ava." She pulled a .38 caliber gun from the drawer and pointed it in Ava's face—

Surprise!

Ava was stunned. "Hold on a second, I—"

"All of you *fucking whores* are the same! Do you think I'm stupid? Do you think I don't know you're *fucking* my husband? I can see it in his eyes every time I mention *your name!*"

"Michelle. Please—"

Her lips quivered. "Don't bother lying to me! I saw your cell phone number on his caller ID, you *home wrecking bitch*!"

"Michelle, I—"

"Then I find out from Lilly you keep calling him at the office. And when he came home last week after staying out all night, I could smell your whorey perfume and cigarette smoke all over him!"

Ava realized the gig was up. "Michelle, I never wanted to hurt you," she said in her native accent.

"Wow. You're not even from Georgia *are you*? You're a fucking liar! Just like he is! And then you have the nerve to get knocked up and try to become my friend so you can take my place? Never! I will *never* let some cunt like you give birth to my husband's child. I'll kill you first!"

"Michelle! Calm down. You have it *all wrong*. I can't even have children."

"Stop fucking lying to me!" Michelle lunged closer.

Ava changed her tune. "You have no idea *who* the fuck I am or what I am capable of. So you better back the fuck down before someone gets hurt."

The phone RANG in the kitchen. Michelle trembled.

Ava stared straight into the gun barrel without moving a muscle. "You picked the wrong cunt to fuck with, Michelle. I can assure you of that."

The phone RANG again. Michelle answered it abruptly, still holding the gun.

"Yes, Wesley."

"Hey, you okay? I'm worried about you."

"Don't be. Everything's fine." Her finger tightened on the trigger.

"Are you sure? You sound weird."

"I'm fine, Wes, take your time." She looked into Ava's hypnotic eyes. "I've got a few things I need to do before you come home, so no need to rush."

"Okay, I'm finishing up here soon…I'll see you in a while." He hung up the phone.

The dial tone played.

Michelle's face crumbled as she spoke back to the empty line. "I love you too, baby." The phone fell from her hand as she sobbed, water dripping down her leg.

Holy shit, her water broke!

Ava took advantage of the situation and lunged for the gun, easily pulling it out of Michelle's hand – throwing it to the floor.

Michelle quickly regained her strength, punching and scratching Ava. "You evil bitch!" she screamed wildly.

Refusing to fight a pregnant woman, Ava held onto Michelle's flailing arms, letting her exhaust herself in the struggle.

Michelle fought back with all her might. As the amniotic fluid gushed down her leg, she twisted and twirled, breaking free, trying to pull Ava down to the floor with her. She bent backwards, slipped on a puddle of fluid on the tile… and

BAAAM!

The back of her skull hit the blunt corner of the granite countertop. And just like that – only hours from giving life – Michelle's body fell to the floor with a THUD.

The room was eerily silent. It felt as if all the birds outside had stopped singing at once.

Ava bent over to feel her pulse.

Nothing.

"*Shit.*"

In her mild panic, she pulled out the large item from her pocket – a blue baby rattle with a bow around it – and placed it on the counter. She grabbed the cordless phone, struggling to remember a number by memory. *404-501-???...Dammit.*

Finally, she remembered. "Hey, it's me. There's a serious change in plans." She glanced at the lifeless body on the floor then towards a knife block on the counter top. "No, I need you to send them here *right now.*"

She hung up the phone.

She pulled a small paring knife out of the wooden block.

She bent down and lifted Michelle's black blouse, covering her face.

Her stretch-marked belly was now fully exposed.

She placed her hand over the bulging torso.

Just then, baby T.J. kicked back...making her smile.

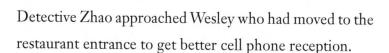

Detective Zhao approached Wesley who had moved to the restaurant entrance to get better cell phone reception.

"Everything good at home, Wes?"

Wesley hung up the phone. "Yes, everything's fine. Please go on."

Zhao slugged the rest of his beer and placed the empty bottle on a dinner table beside him. "Well, there are still too many unanswered questions. For example, why did your mother wait fifteen years to pay Ava? Why not pay her off right away and be done with it?"

"I guess my mother wanted to stretch it out so my father wouldn't notice the money was missing."

"But the cash came from her family trust account. I doubt your father even has access."

Wesley shrugged. "Look, Detective Zhao, avoiding public disgrace meant more to my mother than anything else in the world. Maybe by spreading out the payments she made sure Ava wouldn't go back on her word."

"But here's what really gets me, Wesley. Why would Ava *agree* to wait that long? What was in it for her?"

"*That* I don't know. The whole arrangement was between them…" He pulled out a chair and sat down. "More importantly, have you found any evidence yet? Like DNA or fingerprints proving she's behind this? How long do we have to wait?"

Zhao's eyes darkened. "Wesley, I went to *Le Masquerade* last night. I showed your picture to one of the waitresses there, and you know what she said? She said that you and *her girlfriend*, *Ava*, left the club together and had a threesome at their place Tuesday night."

Wesley's face froze mid-sentence.

"Goddammit. I hate to be lied to—"

"Wait a second, Ava *made me* go there, and without my knowledge she drugged my—"

Zhao pounded his fist. "Maybe I was looking at the wrong Scarborough all along! Your father's not the only person to benefit from your mother's death. Were you aware that she changed her will two months ago? That thirty million dollar trust fund now passes directly *to you!*"

Wesley was taken aback. "Whoa, you are on the wrong track, Detective. You don't know what you're talking about—"

"It's a brilliant plan. Kill your mother, send your father to jail, and you – the only child – walks away with everything. And who better to help you than the woman who hates your mother more than life itself. But you two little lovebirds had one problem: the friends who knew about your past together. So you wiped them out and now you're trying to get rid of your girlfriend by pinning the *whole thing* on her."

"My God. You have this all wrong."

Zhao's body pitched forward. "I hate to be fucked like a bitch, Wesley!"

"This is bullshit. I'm out of here."

"I'm on you like white on rice, boy. You better watch it!"

Wesley approached the exit, then turned around one last time. "You know, you probably should have stayed on the rape beat because your instincts here *are all wrong!*"

He stormed out the door.

Zhao remained. And judging by the faces of the dinner patrons surrounding him, the entire restaurant overheard his dramatic Shakespearean soliloquy.

"Sorry. Please resume your eating. No problems here."

Meanwhile, outside, Wesley dug through his pockets and pulled out a small key – the one that opens his top-secret desk drawer.

Shit, I gave Michelle my car keys.

He stepped out into the light drizzling rain and hailed a red gypsy taxi.

Zhao drove his Ford Crown Victoria along the city streets, struggling to find the missing piece of the puzzle. *Come on, Ava. Why would you wait fifteen years? And you, Miriam. What were you so afraid of? Come on ladies, tell Big Daddy the truth...*

He thought back to his argument with Wesley at the bar...

"You know, you probably should have stayed on the rape beat because your instincts here *are all wrong!*"

He thought back to a night years ago...one of the many nights he'd sat in a hospital room with his good friend, Doctor Jennifer Morris...

A younger Zhao pulled out his notebook. "So, what do we know?"

"Well, we only know three things at this point. Her name is Ava DeSantis, she's a student at Anniston University and she's originally from Atlantic City. I was able to locate her father earlier today, so he's on plane right now."

"Who brought her in?"

"Two of her classmates. They were acting very strange. They said they found her lying naked in the road, next to her car, but my gut tells me they're lying."

Zhao leaned in closer, examining the mummy-wrapped body. "They really screwed this one up, didn't they?"

"You have no idea."

"All right. Just call me if she ever wakes up."

"Absolutely."

Back in the car...

Zhao jolted in his seat. *The statute of limitations for rape is fifteen years!*

"You lying, little prick!"

He quickly turned the car around, screeching his tires in the process...

And sped off towards Wesley's home in Buckhead.

Wesley was about to reach for the doorbell when he noticed the front door was slightly ajar. *Dammit. I told her to set the alarm.*

He entered his home. It was pitch black.

A strange soft rumbling noise permeated the house. *What is that?*

"Michelle?"

It was so dark, not even a streetlight funneled through a window.

"Michelle? Are you here?"

Something with claws JUMPED on Wesley!

He flipped the lights on. It was a huge black cat.

He grabbed its leg and threw it to the floor.

"Michelle!"

Dozens of gray, black and orange cats filled the foyer, meowing together like a chorus of evil waiting for their master to arrive.

He rushed into the bedroom. More cats.

"Michelle! Where are you?"

He charged back into the living room. More cats.

"Michelle!!! Answer me!"

His heart was now in his stomach, fearing the absolute worst.

He slowly walked into the kitchen...

There he saw five tiny white kittens...now red-faced and stained...from licking a fresh pool of blood on the floor.

"Oh, my God."

He spotted a wide blood trail leading into the walk-in pantry.

God, NO!!!

He approached the pantry door...

His heart pounding harder and harder as the chorus of cats meowed louder and louder.

Tears rolled down Wesley's pale, stone face.

"Michelle?"

He reached for the door and gently pushed it open...

And there lay his wife's butchered cadaver on the floor...Her legs bound together with rope...Her midsection ripped opened like a cored out tomato...Her pink and tan organs lying beside her...There was no fetus. Only a discarded placenta and umbilical cord remained.

"NOOOOOOOOOOOO!!!!"

He dropped to the floor, unable to move.

Lying there, breathless, until his anger consumed him.

His lust for vengeance powering him off of the floor.

He ran back into the kitchen.

He picked up the gun.

He leapt over the cats, grabbed his keys and ran out the entrance...

Leaving the door to his home – and his entire life – wide open.

———— ✺ ————

Detective Zhao yelled into his police radio. "I need you to send a squad car to the sex club on Fourteenth and Belvedere, and demand a home address for one their employees. It's an emergency. Her life is in danger."

"What's the name?"

"First name Alpha, Victor, Alpha last name Delta, Echo, Sierra…"

———— ✺ ————

Wesley barged into the marbled lobby of Ava's building. He held the gun tightly in his tweed coat pocket as he walked briskly towards the elevator landing.

"Sir! You need to check in first, " said Lucky the doorman.

Wesley stopped. "I'm in a rush. It's an urgent matter."

"I'm sorry. Building policy. All visitors must check in."

Wesley recognized him. "Wait. Don't I know you from somewhere?"

"Yes, sir. I was here the last time you visited."

"No, that's not it."

"I bet you're here to see Miss Ava in penthouse C again. In fact, I just saw her go up a few minutes ago." Lucky grabbed the visitor log. "Can I get your last name?"

Wesley was explosive. "Scarborough."

Lucky looked down the visitor log. "Let me check the pre-approved visitor list..."

Wesley looked up at the security cameras. Nothing would stop him.

"Okay, here you are, sir. Please go ahead."

Wesley was confused, but played along. "Is Julie up there?"

"I'm not sure. I haven't seen her in a while."

"Thanks."

Wesley left the concierge desk and calmly walked to the elevators. As soon as the doors shut, his blue eyes turned stone grey.

When he arrived on the fifty-third floor, he charged down the hallway to penthouse C.

The door was wide open. He carefully walked inside and saw Ava wearing a long yellow nightgown, sitting with her legs up in a chair, sipping iced tea out of a champagne glass.

"I was beginning to think you forgot where I lived."

"You *insane bitch*."

"Troubled? Yes. Insane? *No*."

Wesley pulled the gun out of his pocket and pointed it directly at her. "Why did you kill my wife? Where is my son?"

"You're beginning to sound like a reporter, Wesley. Let's see, in response to your first question, one would consider her guilty by association—"

"You *bitch!*"

CLICK. A mysterious person in the guest bedroom locked the door.

"I'm not going to hurt you, Julie! Just stay in there!"

"And in response to your second question—"

"Where the fuck is my baby?"

"If you pull that trigger you will never find out. Will you?"

Wesley screamed a primal yell...slammed the gun to the floor and charged at Ava.

Ava leapt up from the chair and ran upstairs.

Wesley followed her, furiously grabbing at her ankles, ripping her long nightgown along the way. At the top of the stairs, Ava broke free and ran to the terrace outside. She kept running and running until there was nowhere else to go. Wesley finally tackled her to the concrete floor. On the way down, he punched her hard once in the face.

Ava smiled, casually wiping the blood from her mouth. "You want to know where your baby is?"

"Yes!"

The air was thick with animal energy.

"Then next time, check the bathtub."

"You. Fucking. Bitch!!!"

Wesley put his hands around her throat, pounding the back of her head against the hard concrete terrace BAM! BAM! BAM!

She grinned back insanely, unmoved by the pain.

He strangled her harder, thrusting his body in a sexual motion.

He pushed his thumbs deeper and deeper against her throat with all of his might.

Ava peacefully accepted her fate as life began to escape her...Her large woodsy-green eyes staring right into his soul.

"Just – like – old – times," she said in between choking breaths.

In an instant, Wesley's reality changed...

His mind flashed back to the night of the rape. Her hallow eyes peering right through him. Her face broken and bleeding.

Wesley was paralyzed. He immediately released his grip and rolled off her body...he sat upright, desperately trying to catch his breath.

Ava crawled passed the garden toward the end of her balcony...hacking and coughing the entire way. She extended her arm and pulled herself up by the railing.

Wesley was immobilized, wailing for his dead wife and baby. Sobs of guilt overtook his body, causing him to fold over with unimaginable pain.

It was his fault. Everything. He had destroyed every single person he loved.

Ava climbed up the cast iron railing...flowing in the wind like a yellow angel...preparing to jump to the end of her days.

"Good-bye, Wesley."

He peeked his head up, seeing she was about to jump.

"Wait! Ava, don't!"

Her long blonde hair danced in the wind like the cover of a romance novel.

"You will always be my first love, Wesley."

"Ava! No—"

"Maybe next time, we'll get it right."

"NOOOOOOO!!!"

Despite his plea, Ava leapt backwards – like a phoenix spreading her wings – and flew down into the night.

The wind growled in her absence…

As Wesley melted to the floor, still smelling her perfume beside him.

CRASH!!!

Someone hit a vase as they rushed in downstairs. Within seconds, three police officers were on the terrace surrounding Wesley.

"Hold it right there!"

Wesley put his hands high in the air.

Detective Zhao walked in from behind the policemen. "Where's Ava?"

Wesley bowed his head, overwhelmed with tremendous guilt.

Zhao rushed over to the railing. He looked down fifty stories and saw the yellow nightgown face down on the street below, surrounded by dozens of pedestrians murmuring at the horrific scene.

"Jesus Christ. Bring him over here."

The police officer handcuffed Wesley, then walked him to Zhao by the railing.

"What happened, Wesley?"

Silence.

"What did you do to her?"

Silence.

"I've got all night to ask questions, Wesley."

Wesley finally imploded…"I pushed her," he blurted. "I pushed her over the edge!"

Zhao was surprised. "Are you sure you want to say that or do you want me to wait for your lawyer?"

Wesley looked down in shame. "She's dead – they're all dead – *because of me*." His face grimaced as tears rolled down his face.

"I already know all about it, Wesley. I just came from your home," he said in a sympathetic tone. "You can fill me in on the details later."

Despite his tremendous pain, Wesley instantly felt a lightness enter his body. Telling the truth after all of these years somehow lifted his heavy soul.

"You have the right to remain silent. Anything you say, can and will be used against you in a—"

"Wait. There's something else."

"Go ahead."

"Go into my front pocket. The right one."

"Why?"

"It's a key. To the top drawer of my office desk."

Zhao raised his brow. "And what will I find in there, Wesley?"

"Something that gets rid of the 'he said, she said shit.'"

Zhao looked at him with heart-felt pity. "All right, let's go."

Police vehicles, ambulances and gawkers flooded the street.

Zhao gently placed Wesley in the back seat of a squad car when a young rookie cop rapidly approached him.

"Detective Zhao, do you need me to get crime scene up there? There's only two crews tonight so it may take a while."

"No, don't bother. We've got a confession."

"But, sir, regulation—"

"Like I said, *this case is closed*, Ramsey. Go find another problem to solve."

———

Lucky the doorman stood next to a forensics worker. The man held the zipper of a black body bag on a stretcher. "Are you sure there's no one else that can do this?"

Lucky was nervous. "Yes, sir. She's got no family. No friends neither. Just me. I'm listed as her emergency contact for the building."

"Are you ready? It's not a pretty sight."

"Yes, sir. I am"

The forensics worker unzipped the body bag to reveal a woman's mangled face…Her black bobbed hair and petite features showed through dislocated flesh and bone.

"Yes, sir. That's Ava DeSantis."

But in reality, it was Julie the waitress!

"Are you sure?"

Lucky nodded his head with sorrow. "Yes, sir. That's definitely Miss Ava."

"Okay, we'll need you to come down tomorrow morning and fill out next of kin paperwork."

"Yes, sir. Whatever I need to do."

The forensics worker re-zipped the bag.

After recovering from the ordeal, Lucky looked at the worker once again, tilting his head. "Call me crazy, but didn't you used to work at the deli in Winn-Dixie?"

Detective Zhao entered his Crown Victoria alone. He shut the door, drowning out the sounds of police chatter behind him. He looked at himself in the rear view mirror. His spikey black hair, small squinty eyes and dimples smiled ear to ear.

"You still got it, Zhao...you still *got it.*"

Lucky the doorman walked along an empty street, away from the fading crime scene behind him. The police cars, ambulances all preparing to leave in the background...

He passed a shiny black conversion van on his right...

He continued walking, up to a black stretch limo parked directly in front of it.

A mysterious man inside the limo rolled down the window.

"It's all done, sir," said Lucky to the mysterious man.

"Good. Did you have any problems?"

"No, sir. We're all set."

The man's arm extended out of the window, handing Lucky two sets of keys. "The red keys are for the van."

Lucky gazed at the van, smiling.

"And the other ones are to the penthouse. Enjoy."

Lucky showcased his wide gap-toothed smile. "Thank you, Mr. Scarborough."

Thomas leaned out the window. "No, Lucky, thank you." His face as refreshed as a newborn man. "Now your Auntie already has keys to the house, so she's all set there. Just be sure to tell her I'm gonna miss those dumplings!"

"I will, sir."

"And tell her thanks for everything. Especially for the introduction."

Ava beamed in the seat across from Thomas, still wearing her yellow nightgown and bungee cord harness...cuddling a wrapped newborn baby in her arms.

Thomas looked at Ava with tremendous love in his eyes.

Lucky stuck his head into the limo. "Good-bye, Miss Ava."

"Call me Julie! I need to get used to it," she said with a smile.

"And take good care of that handsome new son of yours."

"I sure as hell will, Lucky. Thank you."

Lucky pulled back from the limo and waved good-bye.

Thomas lifted his chest and addressed the limo driver: "Gentlemen!"

The black driver panel came down to reveal the white and black biker dudes sitting up front. "Yes, Mr. Scarborough?" they said in unison.

"Your furniture deliverin' days are over, boys. Rio de Janeiro, here we come!"

They all erupted with laughter, enjoying the celebration.

"Oh, I almost forgot," Thomas moved over next to Ava. "I had these made yesterday." He pulled a set of documents out of his interior coat pocket: a social security card, driver's license and passport – all with Ava's beautiful picture and the name *Julie Scarborough*.

He then handed her a red Cartier ring box and a marriage certificate to go with it.

"We got married yesterday too."

"We did?"

"And we'll do it for real on our new private beach."

Ava jokingly wrinkled her brow. "Only if you let me wear yellow."

Thomas scoffed. "So *demanding* already..." He chuckled then gave her a long, deep cinematic wedding kiss that lit up both of their souls.

Afterwards, Ava looked down at the baby, sharing her moment of pure joy.

Barely able to open his eyes, Baby T.J. managed to look back at his mother like she was the only thing that would ever matter in this world.

CHAPTER 31

The Ides Of March

WEDNESDAY, MARCH 15, 2006
1:14 PM

A beautiful woman with long, flowing, dark brown hair stood on the doorstep of Scarborough Mansion. She was wearing a stylish yellow leather coat and carrying a single suitcase.

Eloise opened the door wearing her traditional maid uniform. "Ava?"

"Miss Eloise?"

"Nice to meet you, honey. Please come in."

Ava stepped inside, impressed by the colossal white and gray marbled foyer.

"Thank you for agreeing to come here. Did you have a good flight?"

"Yes, I did. Thank you. I've never flown first class before, it was wonderful."

Eloise smiled. "That's my Thomas. Everything has to be *first class*."

"How sweet."

"He's waiting for you in the library."

Eloise walked Ava down a short hallway lined with antique Civil War era paintings.

"Will Miriam be joining us?"

"No, she's visiting her sister in Maryland." Eloise stopped and leaned into a whisper. "I think it's best if we all keep this little meeting to ourselves."

"Of course."

Eloise winked back. "Good."

In the library, Thomas sat in his favorite high-back chair reading the *Atlanta Journal-Constitution.*

"Excuse me, Thomas. Miss Ava DeSantis is here to see you."

His distinguished brown eyes rose up from the paper…

Ava extended her hand. "Pleasure to meet you, Judge Scarborough."

Thomas dramatically threw the newspaper to the floor. He rose from the chair, grabbed Ava's soft hand and kissed the top of her wrist…

"No, Miss DeSantis. The pleasure is *all mine.*"

EPILOGUE

And that is the story of how my beautiful daughter met her wonderful husband...

And how a runaway girl from Ohio, suffering each day with terminal brain cancer, loved my daughter enough to give up her last two months on earth so she could start a brand new life.

Now *that* my friend, is true bravery.

And years later, after Thomas's death at the age of ninety-three, my handsome grandson took over the family business, becoming the largest manufacturer of Brazilian wood furniture in the world...

Taking a Portuguese beauty queen as his wife, and raising three amazing boys of his own...

And for the little girl I left behind so young, my beautiful, baby girl, Ava.

Who still in her old age spends countless hours in the garden playing with *her* grandchildren, loving and nurturing them just as much as those beautiful yellow roses...

For I have never left you, I have been here all along. Watching you and loving you, feeling your joy and pain through every moment. And like the phoenix that burned before flying away from the ashes of hell, I watched it all, and never once left your side.

Always here, Ava.

Eternally grateful and forever proud to call you *my daughter*.

THE END

AUTHOR MESSAGE

After spending years as a screenwriter in Hollywood, I made the life-changing decision to move into the literary world so I could tell my stories directly to you – the audience – without interference from directors, producers or studio executives. And I can tell you from this first experience of writing a novel that *I am here to stay.*

If you enjoyed reading this book as much as I did writing it, please take the time to share your thoughts on your favorite book review websites like Amazon, Barnes & Noble and Goodreads… Honestly, it would mean the world to me!

The greatest gift you can give an author is to take the time to write an honest review about their book. Reviews are what make or break a book, no matter what the topic or genre.

I have a number of novels lined up over the next several years and would love to stay in touch. Please visit www.MyloCarbia.com to sign up for my VIP READER LIST to learn more about upcoming releases, book signings and giveaways, or follow me on social media:

Twitter: @MyloCarbia
Facebook: AuthorMyloCarbia
Instagram: @mylocarbia
Goodreads: mylo_carbia

Until Next Time,

Mylo Carbia

THE QUEEN OF HORROR

Media Contact

If you are a member of the press or publishing community and would like to schedule Mylo Carbia for:

- Media Interviews
- Book Signings
- Public Appearances
- Blog Tours
- Speaking Events

Or if you are a book reviewer and would like to get on our Advance Reader Copy list to receive pre-release copies of Ms. Carbia's novels, please contact us today:

(310) 873-3645   Contact@EllisonPR.com

Coming Soon

VIOLETS ARE RED

www.VIOLETS-ARE-RED.com